CHANGING

his game

A GAMERS NOVEL

MEGAN
ERICKSON

Entangled Publishing, LLC
2614 South Timberline Road
Suite 109
Fort Collins, CO 80525
Visit our website at www.entangledpublishing.com.

Brazen is an imprint of Entangled Publishing, LLC. For more information on our titles, visit www.brazenbooks.com.

Edited by Heather Howland
Cover design by Heather Howland
Photography by Shutterstock

Manufactured in the United States of America

First Edition April 2105

ENTANGLED
BRAZEN

To all the nerdy boys in my life, and to the best of them all—
the one I married.

Chapter One

Marley Lake hated the spinning rainbow wheel.

Of course, she was all for rainbows. Her favorite show as a kid was *Rainbow Brite*. She even tried to color her cat's tail with Kool-Aid and draw a star on his forehead with markers to make him look like Starlite.

The cat wasn't amused, and Marley's mom took her markers away for a week. *And* her Kool-Aid.

But the spinning rainbow wheel on her Mac? She hated it. It should be a spinning wheel of fire because that was how much she wanted to send it to hell.

Marley growled in the back of her throat and slammed the mouse down onto her desk. Behind that stupid rainbow that she wanted to kill with fire was the layout for the article on the success of the movie *Aric's Revenge*, based off the wildly popular video game. It taunted her. *I'm not finished and you didn't save me, you dumbass.*

She glanced at the clock. Deadline was in forty-five

minutes. She had until eight p.m. to resize the headline, write a subhead to replace the *lorem ipsum* placeholder, and drop the art in place.

She'd been screwing around on social media, waiting for the graphics department to provide the main art. Then her email had pinged with the file she'd been waiting for and that was when her computer locked up.

Of fucking course.

And that rainbow wheel continued to taunt her.

Why hadn't she delegated this to her staff? *Because you need to be in control*, the voice in her head said. Marley ignored it.

She loved her position at *Gamers*, a quarterly magazine with hefty subscription numbers, which was respected in the industry for reviews and news. Marley was head of the copy editing team and took pride in working in the trenches with her employees.

She glanced around at the empty desks. Okay, so she was alone in the trenches today.

Whatever.

Marley hated calling IT. The guy assigned to her department was a sixty-five-year-old guy with a comb-over named Abraham. And he smelled like cheese. She thought about trying to fix it herself but worried she'd dig herself further into the hole.

"Trouble there, Marley?" A voice said over her shoulder and she rolled her eyes before turning around to face her nemesis.

Jack Sorrel.

He wore his ugly herringbone suit jacket and held his bag in one hand and keys in the other. His eyes honed in on her computer, and then he glanced at his ugly white watch. "Deadline's in forty-five minutes."

She narrowed her eyes. "I'm aware of that, Sorrel."

A smirk. "Better get IT on the horn, Lake."

He was surely relishing this. He angled for her job so hard, and his strategy was to shove his head so far up the editor's ass, Marley was surprised he hadn't fully disappeared.

Refusing to let him see her sweat, she swiveled her chair casually and picked up the phone, pressing the button to call her last resort.

"IT, how can we help you?" said the receptionist.

Marley tucked a strand of hair behind her ear. "It's Marley Lake from the copy desk, I…"

Jack walked toward the front doors, chuckling. Marley glared at his back.

"Ms. Lake?" said the voice on the line.

She focused on the phone call. "Oh sorry. Um…is anyone still there to help me out? My computer froze with unsaved work and I have a deadline in less than an hour."

The clicking of nails on a keyboard sounded over the line, some movement, and then deep murmurs. The receptionist came back online. "Someone will be right over, Ms. Lake."

"Thank you," she mumbled, and hung up the phone.

She picked up a package of pretzels and nibbled on them as she swung back and forth in her chair, staring at that stupid rainbow wheel.

She could be at home on the couch eating ice cream. She could be having drinks with her brother. She could be at the gym, sweating her ass off on the treadmill while watching *The Real Housewives of Atlanta* reruns. But instead she sat at her desk, munching on stale pretzels and staring at work she should have given to one of her employees.

Her dedication and work ethic were how she'd moved through the ranks of this male-dominated industry. Marley kept rigid control of her own work and that of her staff. And sometimes, that meant doing a bulk of it herself. It was exhausting. But she loved her job, and she was damn proud of herself. So this was the way it was. She'd made her bed, and now she had to lay in it. She was alone, but at least she had 1800 thread count sheets.

Her phone beeped a text. She leaned over and glanced at the display.

Chad.

It was like he knew.

Come to Bubba's, the text said.

She typed back. *I told you I won't ingest anything from a place named Bubba's.*

Snob.

Degenerate.

Princess.

Peasant.

She smiled as she waited for the next text. Nothing like sibling banter to bring her mood up.

You still at work?

You know it.

You need a hobby.

You need a job.

She cringed because that last text of hers had been a little low.

I'm working on it, the next text said.

I love you, she typed.

I love you too.

Marley placed her phone beside her keyboard as a shadow fell over the desk. She sucked in a breath, prepared to hold it or breathe through her mouth for the next half hour or so to endure Cheese Stink Abraham.

But with that deep breath she inhaled a clean, delicious scent, with just a hint of something spicy, and definitely masculine.

A khaki-clad hip leaned on her desk, and she looked up.

There was no cheap patterned tie or comb-over or anything libido-killing like that.

Nope. It was *him*. The man she'd nicknamed DB for Dark and Brooding. Her fatigued brain whirred to life. What was he doing here? Next to her? She didn't think he worked for the IT department. She'd always assumed he worked for one of the other businesses in the industrial complex where *Gamers'* offices were located.

In fact, maybe he should have been GDB for Gorgeous, Dark, and Brooding. He had to be out of a video game because surely a man who looked like that could only be imaginary.

She muffled a snort at her own lame line. He stood with his arms crossed over his broad chest, the sleeves of his button-down chambray shirt rolled up to his elbows, revealing veined forearms. He wore no tie, and the top couple buttons were undone, so she caught a hint of a V-neck white undershirt and a tantalizing peek at the valley between his pectorals.

She didn't let her gaze drop any further, because his pelvis was in front of her face as she sat at her desk. No way would she be caught staring at his khaki-covered package.

Okay, one peek.

Her mouth watered.

She jerked her eyes back up to his face and thought she might have to go to Bubba's anyway, get really drunk, and then maybe laid, because this was ridiculous.

She cleared her throat. "Um, are you…here for me?"

His face showed nothing. No twitch of those full lips, just an impassive mask. She resisted squirming under his gaze.

"Um, to help me with my computer?" *Or to help me with my orgasm?* she thought.

A nod to her spoken question. Unfortunately.

He had short dark hair and a prominent brow that threw his eyes into shadow from the overhead light. He tilted his head, and she got the first glimpse of his eyes. They were an incredible blue-green color.

She stared at him a minute and then shook herself, turning away from his gaze. And fuck, that was hard to do, like she was swimming against the current.

She waved a hand at her monitor. "So my computer froze and I'm not sure why. And I need to get back to my layout because…" She blushed. "I didn't save it before my computer froze."

She stared at her screen, eyeing his hip in her peripheral vision. He didn't move.

"So yeah," she continued. "All I have is this stupid spinning rainbow—"

"Beach ball."

She jerked her head up to look at him, and it was a relief to float along in his gaze rather than fight to swim away. This was the first time she'd ever heard him speak, and his voice was low and soft.

"Excuse me?"

Those beautiful eyes flicked to her screen and then back to her face. "It's often called a beach ball."

Those eyes. She frowned as she tried to recall what they were talking about. "What's called a beach ball?"

One twitch of his lips. In the right corner. She totally saw it. "The...spinning rainbow...is often referred to as a beach ball."

He said *spinning rainbow* with imaginary air quotes. And he smelled really good. Did he realize how good he smelled? Did he realize how ridiculously good-looking he was? This wasn't *Zoolander*. This was real life.

Good God, she needed this whole thing over with so she could... Oh, who was she kidding? She wouldn't go to Bubba's. She'd go home to her vibrator, B.O.B.

She exhaled and looked back at her screen. "Okay, so I got this beach ball, and if you can pop a pin in it and deflate the fucker, I'd be really grateful." She was too tired for tact.

He didn't move. She stared at her lap and brushed some stray pretzel crumbs off of her skirt. Could she get any sexier? Using words like *fucker* while covered in salt?

Finally he leaned down, and her eyes fluttered closed... she felt her lashes on her check and that was really weird. She wasn't an eyelash-fluttering, butterfly-belly damsel in distress.

Okay, so she was in distress but she only needed to be saved from a beach ball.

See? Totally sexy.

She nibbled her lip and opened her eyes, and his gaze, that beautiful stormy, gold-flecked gaze, was honed in on her mouth. She released her lip, and she swore he made some sort of sound in the back of his throat.

"So, where's Abraham?" she asked.

His eyes returned to hers. "He doesn't work here anymore."

She frowned. "Are you his replacement?"

He hummed, a low rumble. "Something like that."

So he was going to be here more often? She didn't know if she could handle that. "I'm Marley Lake." She licked her lips, and his eyes dipped again. "Nice to meet you."

"Pleasure, Ms. Lake. I'm Austin."

He'd called her Ms. Lake. That did something weird below her belly. She looked at his left hand, checking it for a ring, because that's what you did when you were twenty-seven and unmarried and your mom had an "I love my Grandcat" bumper sticker slapped on her car just to shame her daughter.

No ring. Not even a shadow or a tan.

He turned his eyes to her monitor and placed his hand on her mouse. She wondered if he could feel the heat from her hand on the plastic, the grooves of her fingers. She wondered if he liked it.

She kept her gaze on the screen as the spinning rain—beach ball moved across her desktop.

He moved fast, faster than her eyes could keep up with, pulling up windows and typing things and generally acting like the silent, irritated IT guy that Jimmy Fallon used to play on *Saturday Night Live*. It was kind of cute.

Until she remembered something.

Something *really* important.

She opened her mouth to protest...to do *something* because she'd forgotten she'd been perusing her Tumblr account. She rarely looked at it at work, because it was her outlet. The place to view her fantasies. She'd looked today, though, just this one time because she'd been bored and frustrated.

But she didn't react fast enough because he clicked on her Internet tab and pulled up Tumblr.

Her whole body flushed hot.

There, on the screen, taking up the whole damn thing was a porn GIF. She'd seen it dozens of times and reblogged it dozens of times. Because it was hot. *So* hot.

Black and white. A woman in a black lace bra and black thong with a garter belt and thigh-highs stood in front of a mirror. Her head was thrown back, resting on the shoulder of the man behind her. He was shirtless and in a pair of suit pants. She couldn't see the front of his pants but she liked to imagine they were unbuttoned, his arousal pressed against the woman's crease.

His one hand was wrapped around her throat and the other dipped into the front of her thong. Over and over again, on a loop, his hand slipped beneath the lace, a teasing stroke, as the woman's mouth opened in a silent "o."

She loved the control the man exerted on the woman, and how she relished it. That was what Marley wanted. At the end of the day, in bed, she wanted a man to strip her of the exhausting control she needed to keep at work. She wanted someone else to make the decisions, to be responsible for her pleasure.

Marley squeezed her legs together as sensations raced through her body. She felt an invisible hand at her throat and imagined a long finger dipping into her wetness.

She exhaled harshly. This was fifty shades of inappropriate. Would Austin report her? What had she been thinking looking at this at work?

She shifted her gaze to the side to gauge his reaction. His face was close to the screen, the movement of the GIF passing light and shadow over his face.

She was embarrassed. She was turned on. She was everything all at once. Her stomach flipped over, and she discretely rubbed her damp palms on her skirt.

She must not have been discreet because Austin's head turned toward her, and she braced herself for the look in his eyes.

If it were possible, she would have sizzled like a well done steak under Austin's intense stare.

She swore his nostrils flared but she quickly chastised herself because clearly she'd read too many shifter romances lately. He couldn't...smell her arousal, could he?

She needed B.O.B.

When Austin spoke, his voice was so soft, she barely heard it. "Do you like that?"

She forgot she was at work. She forgot Austin was sort of like a coworker. Because he was staring at her like he wanted to devour her, and that GIF was moving in the corner of her vision, and her whole body was on fire.

Caught under his current, she nodded.

His lips parted and a hot, minty breath escaped them, coasting over her face.

Her heart pounded in her ears, and it sounded like a waterfall. She was teetering on the edge in a raft and barely clinging to shore.

And then the doors of the office banged open. Austin snapped his head up as her irritating coworker, Jack, strode back in. He nodded in their direction. "Forgot my wallet."

Marley watched him as he whistled on his way to his desk, grabbed his wallet out of his top drawer, and then gave her a wave as he left again.

When she looked back at her computer, Tumblr was gone and so was the beach ball. Her design program was back up, her project apparently intact, and Austin clicked save.

He straightened and stepped off to the side of her desk. Away from her.

She barely pulled herself onto the shore. And part of her mourned not taking the plunge.

He didn't say a word, only stared at her, his face back to that impassive mask, like they hadn't just watched some man with his hand down a woman's panties. As if he hadn't asked her in that low, husky voice *if she liked that.*

God, was this her life?

"Thanks," she said, fingers tangled in her hair behind her ear.

A barely perceptible shift in his eyes before he said, "Anytime."

When he turned and walked toward the front doors, she told herself to get back to work, to quit ogling the guy, but the way his shirt shifted across his broad upper back, the way his butt filled out those pants… Oh Lord.

She didn't look back at her monitor until the doors closed behind him.

Chapter Two

Austin Rivers didn't go back to the office. Doug could handle the rest of the shift. It was end of business hours anyway.

He reached his car, a black Jaguar, which he always parked behind the building, and rested his hand on the top of the door. His head slumped forward between his shoulders.

He should have let Doug handle it. It was his shift. His job. Austin shouldn't have even been there, but sometimes he helped out at IT, under the pretense he was just another employee. And he'd happened to be there today, of all days.

He'd heard the receptionist say *Ms. Lake* and maybe he shouldn't have skipped lunch, because he was just light-headed enough to act like a fool and volunteer to help her.

Marley.

She was one of only three women in that office, and she held one of the highest positions at the magazine. She often ate lunch alone on the picnic table right outside of his office, the wind blowing through her curly brown hair, the sun catching on the red highlights.

She usually wore tight pencil skirts that cupped her well-endowed ass, and stockings with a seam up the back with high heels. So many times he'd wanted to trace that seam with his fingers.

He thunked his head on the car. He was a fool.

Because up close, she was even better. Almond-shaped hazel eyes. Creamy, fair skin. A smattering of freckles on her nose.

He'd admired her from afar for her beauty and her brains and ambition. But he'd stayed away because he had no business fraternizing with her.

He realized it was just an assumption, but she seemed the type of woman who liked gentle sex full of sighing and declarations of love. Austin's tastes ran…a little different. Rougher. Dirtier might be a good descriptor, too. Frankly, he liked control everywhere in his life. It was how he'd come to be this successful at thirty-two.

And that need for control carried into the bedroom.

He'd shoved Marley to the back of his mind as best as he could. She never gave off any sort of vibe that she'd be compatible with him in bed in any way.

But that GIF.

He moaned and shifted his hips. He'd been hard ever since he saw that image on her monitor. Since he heard the catch in her throat and saw the blush spread over her cheeks and top of her chest, visible along the V-neck of her shirt.

Marley had been turned on. She'd liked that—the man's hand at the women's throat. Holding her. Claiming her. His hand dipping into her wet folds…

Austin wrenched open the door and dropped into his seat, starting up his car and listening to the purr of the engine. The weather was finally warming up, announcing that spring in Willow Park, Pennsylvania, was in full force. After a particularly long and brutal winter, Austin was happy for it.

He pulled out of the lot and steered toward home. He had to do something to get Marley out of his mind. To relieve this ache. He could call…

He shook his head. No one else would do. He liked specific things and that took a specific woman. A trusting woman. A strong woman.

Like Marley, a voice whispered in his head, and he gunned the engine down the highway. He wondered what other fantasies she had, which made his mind race and his knuckles turn white where they gripped the steering wheel.

His phone rang and he glanced at the display before answering. "Hey, Grant."

"Am I catching you at a bad time?" There was a hint of a smile in Grant Osprey's voice. "Date maybe?"

He was usually amused at his friend's attempts to encourage a social life. Tonight he wasn't. "I'm leaving *Gamers* after checking up on IT. What can I do for you?"

Grant clucked his tongue. "So formal."

"Grant—"

"Can you take Syd to the new movie out tomorrow? That Axel Revenge thing?"

There was a teasing tone to his voice now. It was like Grant couldn't have a conversation without trying to annoy the shit out of Austin. He'd never admit it, but Austin actually liked it.

Grant knew the name of the movie. The magazine they

owned together had reported on it for the last year. And Grant was the only one who knew Austin had spent most of his early twenties creating the video game on which it was based. "*Aric's Revenge.*"

"Oh, is that the name of it?" Still with the teasing tone, but Grant sounded distracted, which wasn't unusual. The man was always completing about five tasks at once, with a side of ADD.

Austin sighed. "*Aric's Revenge*, that's the name of the movie, adapted from the video game of the same name, which sold over fifty million retail copies and made me a very rich man."

A pause. "God, I love when you spout statistics. Gets me hard."

Austin barked out a laugh—a sound he rarely made but one Grant seemed to pry out of him. They'd started *Gamers* magazine together right out of college. Grant was the public CEO, the name everyone knew, while Austin used a pseudonym on most of the paperwork. Only Grant knew that Austin had a secret partnership in *Gamers*, just like he was the only one who knew about *Aric's Revenge*. Austin didn't trust anyone other than Grant to know about him, what he did, how much money he had. He'd been let down too many times, lied to, stolen from. He'd learned his lessons from painful experience.

Grant laughed. "Okay, so I know this is short notice, but I've got this dinner meeting with one of *Gamer's* advertisers and Syd needs a ride. She's meeting her friends, but I'm not comfortable with her riding with a kid who just got her license. So, can you drive her there, watch the movie while she watches it with her friends, and then bring her home?"

Sydney was Grant's fourteen-year-old daughter. He'd had a one-night stand freshman year of college and nine months later, Sydney was born. Her mother had planned to put her up for adoption, but Grant said he'd support the child. So with the help of his parents, Grant secured custody and worked his ass off to support her. It was one of the reasons he and Austin started *Gamers* together. Grant was a great businessman and put a lot of effort into the idea of *Gamers*. But as a recent college graduate ten years ago, he needed some capital to get the magazine off the ground. Austin, whose bank account had been padded with funds when he'd begun working with a software company on *Aric's Revenge*, invested in the magazine. It was important to him to help Grant, since Sydney was like a niece to Austin. "Of course I'll take her."

A muffled sound, then Grant yelling in the distance, "Baby, he'll take you!" Then an excited squeal, which he assumed came from Sydney. "Thanks a lot, man," Grant said into the phone.

"No problem."

"Don't forget about checking—"

"—the ingredients on the boxes of candy because of her peanut allergy."

A pause, then, "You're the best." Austin could hear the smile in his friend's voice.

"I'm almost home. What time do you need me tomorrow?"

"Seven?"

"See you then."

Five minutes later, Austin parked in his garage and pushed the button on the remote on his dash to lower the doors.

Then he leaned his head against the steering wheel.

Taking Sydney to see a movie tomorrow night would be good for him. An action-packed movie should hold his attention. Even if the damn thing made him think of Marley, picturing her sitting at her desk, working on a layout of an article about the movie that was *his* creative vision.

He had to do something to forget about her.

Because even though she didn't know it, even though his ownership in *Gamers* was silent, she was still his employee.

So despite how he ached for her, despite that fucking GIF that taunted him, he needed to keep her in his fantasies. And out of real life.

He was great at maintaining control, but a churning in his gut made him wonder if this would be the one time he'd let it slip.

Marley lay with her head and back on the floor, her feet propped up on the seat of her couch. She wore a sports bra, oversized sweatshirt that hung off one shoulder, and a pair of underwear. She had been doing sit-ups. Then her cat needed petting, then she got distracted by a watermark on the ceiling of her apartment that looked like a penis, and then she zoned out.

She idly scratched Sadie's ears and closed her eyes. Her mind wandered to that GIF of the woman and man, her go-to fantasy, but it was quickly replaced by a pair of sea-green eyes.

She had to stop thinking about yesterday. About him.

Austin. He was a coworker—sort of—and she couldn't get involved. She'd fought hard in this testosterone-filled industry to be taken seriously. She wouldn't let a moment of weakness and this sexual dry spell be her downfall. She couldn't even imagine what the guys in the office would say if they found out she was fantasizing about sleeping with one of the IT guys. Let alone if she actually *did* it.

Fuck.

Her front door opened, and she turned her head. Chad sauntered in, stooping to pet Sadie who'd deserted her for a guy. Figured. The furred turncoat.

"Can't you knock?" she asked.

He held up his key to her apartment. "Why bother?"

Chad wore a pair of leather pants, a tight gray T-shirt, and a leather jacket. The buckles on his motorcycle boots clinked when he walked across her scarred hardwood floor. He wore his hair, which he'd dyed black, in a faux-hawk and his diamond earrings glittered in the light.

They had the same eyes, but Marley always thought they looked better in her little brother's face than her own.

Chad plopped on the couch. Sadie promptly jumped in his lap and curled up in a ball. He wrinkled his nose at Marley. "Go put on some pants."

She looked at her bare legs and tilted her hips. She needed to shave. "These are my workout clothes."

"You're not working out, though. You're staring at your ceiling."

She glared.

"Are you staring at that watermark that looks like a dick? I noticed it the other night when I crashed here."

"Yes!" Marley pointed to it excitedly. "Curves a little to

the left."

"I prefer them a little bent."

Marley rolled her eyes.

He smacked her ankle. "What's up? You get that layout finished?"

She couldn't stop the blush creeping across her face, because the layout made her think of…other things. "Yes."

Chad cocked his head and narrowed his eyes, leaning slightly toward her. "Are you blushing?"

"No."

"You are. Why are you blushing?"

She dug her heel into his thigh and earned a hiss from Sadie. "Stop it."

Chad relaxed back onto the couch and tapped his finger to his chin. "Tell me why you blushed or I'll keep bugging you."

He would, too, the jerk. She released a breath and raised her hands over her head, playing with the ends of her hair spread out on the floor. "There was an incident with the IT guy."

Chad frowned. "Cheese Stink Abraham?"

She snorted. "No, this was a new guy."

Chad raised his eyebrows. "Is he hot?"

Her brother's sexuality was fluid. He always said he was attracted to souls, not gender. And he would absolutely keel over and declare his undying love if he saw Austin. She sighed.

Chad's eyes widened. "No words? Just a sigh? Damn, he must be smoking."

"He saw my Tumblr," she blurted and Chad's smile immediately froze, and then dropped off his face.

"What did you say?"

She stared up at the ceiling, concentrating on the phallic watermark. "My computer froze and he saw my Tumblr account and…"

She looked back at her brother. The only movement was his eyes, blinking rapidly. "Oh my God, he saw your porn."

She covered her face with her hands and groaned. "It was awkward and—"

"Were you turned on?"

She looked at him and bit her lip.

"Was he turned on?"

She bit down so hard she tasted blood. "I think."

Chad dislodged Sadie from his lap and jumped to his feet, then walked over to Marley's bookcase, fingers running over the spines of her books.

"What are you doing?"

"There it is," he muttered. He pulled out a spiral bound sheaf of paper from between a graphic novel and a dog-eared John Grisham paperback.

She braced her weight on her elbows. "Is that my employee handbook?"

He sat down and she climbed off the floor to sit beside him as he ran his index finger down the page of contents. "What are you doing?"

He didn't look up. "Checking to see if there is anything about fraternizing among coworkers."

"Chad—"

"What? You two basically skipped first base and are halfway to second because you've already watched porn together."

She smacked his thigh. "We didn't watch porn together."

He raised an eyebrow at her. Just one. She hated when he did that.

"Ok, so we sort of did," she mumbled.

He grinned and bent his head back to his task. Marley played with Sadie, who was rolling around with a toy at Marley's feet.

She looked up when Chad snapped the handbook shut. "There are no rules about fraternizing that I can see. You are free to screw the brains out of your IT guy."

She gave her brother's shoulder a shove while he laughed. "Just because there's no rule doesn't mean it's okay!"

He tossed the book on her side table. "Why not?"

She twisted her hands in her lap. "Because...because what if people find out? I've worked hard for those guys to take me seriously in that office and then to blow it all by... blowing a coworker?"

He laughed harder.

"Chad!"

He held up a finger and then finally spoke when he caught his breath. "Look, here's the thing. You're telling me they won't take you seriously if you...what? Remind them you're a woman?"

"That's not—"

Chad wasn't laughing anymore. At all. "No, seriously, Marley. I don't understand. He's not a direct coworker. He's an IT guy you'll see in the office, what, once a week? It's not a conflict of interest unless he...I don't know...installs more RAM in your computer than others."

She pursed her lips. He didn't understand because he wasn't a woman.

"Marley, showing interest in a man doesn't make you

weak. It's not going to make those men think any less of you. And if it does? There are discrimination acts in place for that reason. You're a gorgeous twenty-seven-year-old woman who works sixty hours a week. You deserve some happiness."

She stared into those sincere hazel eyes, so like her own. She was conflicted. She'd suppressed herself for so long trying to make it at *Gamers*. She loved her job, so why was she so worried about what her asshole coworkers like Jack thought of her?

"I'm good at my job," she said.

Chad nodded and laid a hand on her knee. "You are."

"Fuck them. I'm a woman, right? I have needs."

Chad kept nodding. "You do." He paused. "So what's this guy's name?"

She ran her tongue along the back of her teeth, savoring the name in her mouth before speaking. "Austin."

Chad's eyes sparkled. "So, Austin can check your software updates, huh?"

Marley rolled her eyes, but Chad wasn't done. "And he can defragment your hard drive?"

"Chad—"

"Perform some pair programming…horizontally?"

"Oh my God, stop now."

Chad had erupted into a fit of laughter again, bent over at the waist. Marley folded her arms over her chest and crossed her legs, jiggling her foot in the air.

When Chad was gasping for breath, she asked, "Are you done?"

"Maybe," Chad breathed. She growled, and he held up his hands. "Okay, okay. Look, I'll make up for my teasing by treating you to a movie. *Aric's Revenge* is out."

That stupid video game, and that stupid movie. But she wanted to see it. She played the game and beat it a week after it came out.

She hopped up. "Fine, but you're paying."

"No problem. Just shave your legs for me, all right? Getting a little cave woman there."

She shot him the finger over her shoulder as she walked down the hall to shower.

Chapter Three

"Quit taking all the red ones," Chad complained, snatching the bag of Sour Patch Kids from Marley's hands.

"Hey!" she protested.

"I bought them."

"Yeah, for me!" She grabbed the bag back and shot him a glare.

Chad leaned back in his seat and took a sip of his gigantic soda as the light of the pre-show slides flickered across his face. The theater was packed. *Aric's Revenge* had been out for a week or two, but the positive buzz seemed to be fueling more ticket sales.

Marley dug in the bag for more coveted red, corn-syrupy goodness and pulled out a couple. She tossed one in her mouth and looked around at the crowded theater.

The movie was set to start in about five minutes, but a couple of patrons trickled in. Her eyes caught on a man and a teenage girl walking down the middle aisle. Something was familiar, and his walk…

"Mars."

She turned at the nickname her brother sometimes used for her. "Yeah?"

"What's the set-up of this movie again?"

She frowned. "How do you not know? You're the one who suggested it."

He shot her a small grin "Nah, I don't know anything about it. I just suggested it because I thought you would like it."

She smiled back. "Aren't you sweet."

"So who's Aric and why does he want revenge?"

She tried to explain it as briefly as she could. The video game was set in a fantasy medieval world. Aric was a warrior, stripped of his knighthood, who was seeking revenge against a king who killed his family and enslaved his wife.

"So, what you're saying is he's a pissed-off motherfucker with armor and a sword."

"And dragons," she said.

"Come again?" Chad asked.

She opened her mouth to answer him but instead of her own voice, she heard a deep, soft one—the same deep voice she'd heard in her head since yesterday afternoon.

"Aric's dragons are summoned when his anger level reaches sixty-seven percent."

Marley stared at Austin, who stood in the aisle by Chad's chair, a teenage girl at his side, nodding her head in agreement.

Austin's gaze was on Marley, even though he answered Chad's question. "It's rather difficult for the player, because he or she must allow Aric to be injured enough to raise his anger level, but not enough to kill him. It's a delicate balance. And then once the proper anger level is achieved, it must be held for five seconds. Of course, the programmers erred and it's more like four-point-seven seconds." His face darkened, like that error really bugged him.

He wore a pair of worn jeans that hung low on his hips, and a dark red henley, one top button undone, the fabric stretched over his chest. He talked like a textbook and looked like an underwear model. The combination did absolutely everything for her libido.

She looked to her brother, who stared at her coworker with eyes the size of saucers. Chad slowly turned his head to Marley, a silent question in his expression.

She cleared her throat and pointed at the man in the aisle. "This is Austin."

Chad, who had just taken a sip of his soda, choked and she elbowed him with narrowed eyes.

Once he regained his breath, he wiped his watery eyes and held his hand out. "Nice to meet you, Austin. I'm Chad, Marley's brother."

Austin mouthed a word silently, and she could have sworn it was *brother*. He turned to the girl at his side. "This is Sydney, my friend's daughter. Sydney, this is Marley and Chad."

The girl smacked her gum. "Yeah, I got their names Unc Aust, but thanks. Nice to meet you!"

Chad motioned to the empty seats in their aisle, next to Marley. "Why don't you guys sit with us?"

Austin looked almost alarmed, and Marley started to shake her head.

"That's perfect!" Sydney said brightly. "I'm sitting with my friends and Unc was going to have to sit all by himself." She rose on her tiptoes and stretched her neck toward her uncle. His eyes on Marley, Austin mechanically bent so she could kiss his cheek.

"Have fun!" Sydney said, and turned to walk away.

Austin reached out a hand and gently gripped her arm. "I checked ahead of time with the theater. They use canola oil on the popcorn, so you can eat that. But the soft pretzels here are a no, okay?" His soft voice held an unmistakable tenderness that hit Marley right in the chest.

Sydney wrinkled her nose. "Really? I thought I could eat the pretzels."

He shook his head. "They changed companies. Sorry, sweetheart."

She sighed. "Oh well." Then she shot him a beaming smile. "Thanks for checking. I wouldn't have thought to ask again."

"Of course, Syd." His fingers squeezed her arm and then he let go. "I'm not sure your father would ever forgive me if I had to shove an Epi-Pen in your thigh in the middle of a movie theater."

Sydney laughed. "It'd be a fun picture for Facebook."

He pointed to the corner of the theater where a loud group of teenagers was pointing and waving at them. "Go join your friends. Text me if you need me."

Sydney waved and trotted away.

Marley was so caught up in the way he treated his friend's daughter, that she almost missed her brother's next words.

"Have a seat right there beside Marley." Chad stood

up with a triumphant grin, and Marley considered sneaking laxatives into his soda. She stood up, too, plastering herself as far back as possible so Austin could walk by. She held her breath, not wanting to smell his intoxicating scent, and then thought, *Fuck it*, because unless she wanted to die from lack of oxygen, she was going to have to breathe throughout the movie anyway. So she inhaled deeply like a weirdo when he walked by.

Austin seemed to avoid touching her as much as she avoided touching him. He sank into his seat, and she closed her eyes, praying for strength as she slipped down into hers.

Chad was still grinning. She ignored him.

Austin craned his head in the direction Sydney had walked, and Marley pretended that it wasn't adorable he brought his friend's daughter to a movie. She pretended he didn't smell like a total dream. She pretended he wasn't the hottest man she'd ever seen in her life.

"So, what's in the pretzels Sydney can't have?" she asked.

"She has a peanut allergy. The new pretzels the theater sells are made in a factory that also processes peanut products, so she can't have them, because her allergy is pretty severe."

He seemed to know a lot about the little girl, and her allergy. "And she calls you Uncle?"

Austin smiled and looked down where his hands gripped his thighs. "Yeah, I've known her dad since I was eighteen. So, I was a presence most of her life. She's like a niece to me."

Could she melt into a pile of goo in the theater? Because that's what she felt like. A big melted, gooey Sour Patch Kid.

The lights dimmed, and Austin straightened as the

previews started. Most of them were for action movies, although a couple were comedies. Austin sat silently, gaze on the screen. And Marley swore he didn't even crack a smile. God, she wanted to see his smile.

When the movie finally started, the screen showed a montage of a younger Aric, chained to a cell as his wife was ripped from his arms.

Marley tried to lose herself in the story, but it was impossible with Austin this close. Sitting in a theater in jeans wasn't comfortable so she had worn a simple sweater dress. She crossed her bare—now shaved—legs so that her foot brushed Chad, not Austin.

She kept her face turned toward the screen but her gaze strayed. Austin's palms were flat on his thighs and his legs were spread. His pinkie on his right hand was close, oh so close. If he extended it an inch or two, he'd brush her bare thigh.

She wanted him to. God, she wanted him to. Her back was tense, and she squeezed her legs together, wishing she'd done something last night to relieve this ache. She hadn't, conflicted with guilt and unease over fantasizing about a coworker. But now, with his scent surrounding her, his soft voice in her ears, she told herself to get a grip.

What was wrong with her?

And then Austin leaned over, and she closed her eyes as the heat of his breath touched her ear. "Aric's motivations are interesting, aren't they?"

She didn't answer, just nodded, because she didn't trust her voice.

"He tracks down every last one of his enemies," he continued. "His goal isn't to rescue his wife, Evelyn. It's to exact revenge, which makes the game aptly titled."

Aptly. He'd used the word aptly in a sentence. Why was that hot? Did she have an SAT fetish? Heat pooled in her belly and a bead of sweat dripped between her breasts. They ached with fullness, and she knew her nipples were hard.

The soft, seductive voice didn't stop. "He becomes so entrenched in his mission that he becomes a monster, not unlike his dragons. It isn't until he's reached the wife of his enemy and has a chance to take her by force, that he realizes he's become exactly what he hated."

She turned her head, so that her lips were an inch away from his. Those eyes flickered in the light of the screen. She somehow found her voice and forced it through her vocal chords. "That's the turning point in the game, when he changes his mission of revenge to one of rescue. He takes back what's his."

His chest rose and fell. "And do you think that's appropriate?"

She could close the distance, just an inch, and those lips would be on hers. What would they feel like? Would he kiss hard or soft? Would he grip her jaw and direct the kiss? "Do I think what's appropriate?"

He licked his lips and she felt the wet heat of that tongue on the edge of her lower lip. "That he takes what's his."

She released a breath, and his eyelids drifted shut.

She needed to leave. She had to get away from him before she hiked up her skirt and straddled him with his friend's daughter, and her brother, and everyone and God as witnesses.

Jerking away from him, she stood up, mumbling, "Excuse me," to a confused Chad. She slipped past him and out of the movie theater.

She dashed out into the lobby and burst into the bathroom. She leaned over the sink and stared at her reflection. The blush on her cheeks extended down her neck and across her chest. Her breasts looked swollen and her eyes glassy. Oh God, she looked drugged.

Drugged on that man with his big words.

He takes what's his.

How much did he interpret from that GIF he'd seen? Did he figure out that fantasy? Because as strong as she portrayed herself in public, in her office, she dreamed of trusting a man like that with her body.

She wanted to lean her head back on a strong shoulder while he held her throat in a perfect grip, the other hand playing her like an instrument, with a rhythm only he knew.

Marley shook her head and splashed cold water on her cheeks, patting them dry with a paper towel. She straightened her dress in the full-length mirror and then took a deep breath.

She could do this. She'd ask Chad to switch seats. She could get through this movie and away from the incredible force that was Austin.

A ustin had to talk to her.

His control was dripping like hot liquid from the ends of his fingers, evaporating before it even hit the ground. He was gone, so far gone, over this woman.

He knew he'd pushed Marley too far but he couldn't resist feeling her out, wondering if that GIF was something she wanted for herself.

Did she imagine herself in that role? Did she want to be that woman, with a strong man's hand around her throat? Playing with her? At his mercy?

He could give that to her. He could fulfill that fantasy.

He shifted from his position outside the bathrooms in the lobby and waited for Marley to emerge. He wasn't worried about Sydney. He'd texted her and told her he'd be in the lobby, and she'd texted back with a winky face. He didn't know what that was for.

The bathroom door opened and Marley walked out, then froze. Like she sensed him. Like a hunted deer. Her chest rose and fell and then her head slowly swiveled until she eyed him, tucked away into a secluded alcove.

He wanted to tell her to come to him, but she had to make the first move. She had more control over him than she thought.

Indecision flashed over her face before her chin lifted in a determined gesture. And then in a couple of swift strides of those long, shapely legs, she was in front of him, gazing up with huge hazel eyes.

"Sydney…?" she asked.

"She's fine," he answered.

She nodded, and her tongue sneaked out to touch the corner of her upper lip. He let his gaze drop. He'd fallen asleep last night thinking about her blushing in her office chair and woken up imagining sinking between her thighs.

And then to see her with another man at the movie? He'd wanted to toss the guy on his ass, so when she'd introduced the man as her brother, the rush of relief had been palpable.

He couldn't resist anymore. He had a plan he'd been

mulling, and he'd come to a decision that morning. He just had to keep his identity secret a little longer.

It was the coward's way, but he wanted her with a bone-deep ache, and if her glazed eyes were any indication, she wanted him too.

Only one more thing to test.

He raised his right hand slowly, waiting to see if she'd flinch, but she didn't. She only stared back at him with those beautiful almond-shaped eyes. He wrapped four fingers around the back of her neck, starting with his pinky and then the rest in succession, like a scale on piano keys. At his touch, she sucked in a breath, the skin of her neck pebbling with goose bumps. He wanted to latch onto it, lave the skin with his tongue until it was smooth again.

He settled his thumb into the hollow of her throat, feeling the pulse beat there and then laid his palm flat on her collarbone.

The flush on her face deepened, her eyes glazed, and her breath escaped between her parted lips in gasps.

He caressed her skin with his thumb. "You like my hand at your throat?"

She didn't answer and doubt crept over him. Maybe he'd misinterpreted, maybe—

"Yes."

The answer was so soft, so barely spoken, that he thought maybe he hadn't heard it. He needed more.

"Say it." His voice was hard, flinty, like the striking of a match.

Her eyelids, which had sunk, fluttered open. "What?"

"Say the words."

A longer pause, but he was more confident this time,

because her body was pliant under his hand.

And when her voice came, it was everything he'd thought it would be. "Yes, I like your hand at my throat."

That was really all he needed. Moving fast, he turned her so that her back was against the wall in the alcove, his body blocking her from view even though no one could see them unless they purposely meant to be there.

Her hands flew to his biceps and rested there. He waited, wanting to give her time to say no, to stop him if he made her uncomfortable. One word and he'd back away, even if it would feel like peeling his skin off.

And then, with her eyes directly on his, she dropped her arms and laid her palms flat on the wall.

The sight of Marley, submitting to his control, her full breasts and hips on display under a thin dress, had his cock swelling and lengthening in his jeans.

It was painful.

But he ignored himself and focused on her. He leaned in and ran the tip of his nose up her neck, angling his head so his tongue followed the same path. Marley sucked in a breath, murmuring, "Austin," in that breathy voice that he wanted to play on repeat.

He couldn't wait anymore. He needed that mouth. And so he took it, tilting her chin so he could delve his tongue between her lips to tangle with her own. She tasted sweet and sour and feminine and he knew he'd never be cured of his desire for her.

Despite her body language, she wasn't passive in the kiss. She nipped at his lips and ran her tongue over his teeth, tasting him while he tasted her.

His whole body was on fire and Marley was the only

thing keeping him from dissolving into ash.

He pulled out of the kiss and placed his lips at her ear. His left hand, which had been clutching her hip, trailed down the outside of her thigh.

"You taste sweet, just like I knew you would, Marley," he breathed into her ear. His fingertips skimmed along the bottom of her dress, and he reveled in the small gasp that escaped from her lips. He tapped a finger on her inner thigh. "Would you taste as sweet here?"

She moaned, the sound torn from her throat and rippling over his skin as she dropped her forehead onto his shoulder.

Her legs trembled beneath his fingers, and he couldn't wait any longer. He had to know. He walked his fingers up her thigh, so she knew exactly what he was doing. So she could pull away or protest.

But she didn't. And when he reached her underwear, he ran one finger along her crease, over the fabric.

Damp.

"My sweet Marley," he purred in her ear, and her whole body shuddered. "You're wet already? Just from the sound of my voice, the touch of my hand at your throat, and the taste of my mouth?"

Her breath heated his shirt at his shoulder, and her back rose and fell with deep breaths.

Her consent came seconds later, a soft sound muffled against his shirt. "Please."

He rotated his right hand so now it cupped the back of her neck, his thumb caressing the vein on the side and keeping her face pressed to his shoulder. And then he hooked her underwear with the thumb of his left hand and delved two fingers into her wetness.

She was soaked, her arousal slippery on his fingers, and he ran his tongue over the lobe of her ear. "Drenched. Could you come from my voice alone?"

Her answer was a low moan, and he thought that would be something they could try another time.

Don't fuck this up, Austin, or there won't be another time.

He found the hard bud of her clit with his thumb and began rubbing in a circle. "Is that what you like?" he whispered in her ear. "A slow rub on that pretty little button? Or do you want my fingers, pumping in and out of your pussy?"

She squeaked. At least, it sounded like a squeak, so he took it as an affirmative and plunged two fingers into her softness. She gasped. "I think both," he answered himself.

He kept up the rhythm, rubbing her hardening, slick clit with his thumb and curling his fingers as he pushed them in and out of her. She was active now, grinding her hips, fucking herself on his hand, small sounds escaping her throat. He gritted his teeth because a couple of shifts of his hips and he would come on her thigh. He refused to do that, because right now was about her.

He kept her face pressed against his shoulder. "Do you want to come, my sweet Marley?" Her only answer was a nod, her whole body shaking and shuddering. "Ride my hand. Take what you want. And *come.*"

She did. On command, just like that, muffling her cries by biting into his shoulder. He latched on to her neck, sucking the skin into his mouth, wanting to mark her.

And then she was finished, her muscles still convulsing around his fingers. He shifted his hand on her neck to push her back against the wall, wanting to see her face.

Her eyes were half-closed, her lips wet and swollen. She

looked debauched.

She looked beautiful.

He pulled his fingers out of her underwear and squeezed her neck slightly, signaling her to look at him. To focus.

She did, her eyes widening as he slipped his index finger and second finger between his lips, sucking on them and then pulling them out of his mouth. He smiled. "I was right. Your pussy tastes just as sweet."

Her breath left her chest in a rush and her eyes dipped down to the front of his pants and then back to him.

He shook his head and pressed a kiss to her lips. "Another time."

Her mouth opened but no sound came out. She swallowed, her throat working under his hand and tried again. "So now I owe you twice."

He chuckled. "Then I guess…another time…twice."

Her gazed bounced around his face before settling on his eyes. "Okay."

Chapter Four

Chad smacked his gum, blew a bubble, and then popped it with his finger. "You wanna talk about why you were in the lobby so long and then came back all flushed and glassy-eyed?"

They were sitting on her living room floor, passing a tube of refrigerated cookie dough between them.

Marley bit down on a chocolate chip and didn't answer. After the movies, she'd changed back into sweatpants. Well, she'd tried to go pants-less but Chad grumbled. He changed into some clothes that he kept there. He would probably sleep on her couch later, too. Hopefully she could convince him to make his stuffed French toast the next day.

"Mars?"

She looked up. Chad raised his eyebrows as he sipped his wine.

Boxed wine and cookie dough. The Lake siblings were pure class.

"Um…"

"Austin left after you did and never came back."

She knew this fact. After their…encounter, he'd told her he planned to stay in the lobby to wait for Sydney. Marley had asked if he wanted to see the rest of the movie. He'd shrugged and said he knew how it ended.

And she'd walked away.

Her cheeks heated as she remembered when she had completely lost her marbles and allowed him to bring her to orgasm with his fingers in a fucking movie theater lobby.

Again, pure class.

Chad's eyebrows were still raised. Maybe if she didn't answer, they'd stay that way forever. She sighed. "We made out."

Chad's eyebrows rose higher and she marveled at his ability to contort his face. "You made out?"

"Yeah."

"Where?"

She picked at a hole in her sweatpants. "In the lobby."

"Holy shit."

"Mm hmm."

Chad leaned back on his hands. "He is super hot, even if he talks like my senior biology teacher."

Marley snorted.

"Well," Chad patted her knee. "Good for you. You need to let go a little."

"I know. And it was…" Her cheeks heated again. "Amazing. But I owe him." A giggle burst from her lips and she waggled her eyebrows at Chad.

"Yeah, okay, no more details."

"But I don't have time for a relationship."

Her brother cocked his head. "Who said anything about that? Just have fun with a hot guy for once in your life, Mars. A guy who can get you off. Enjoy the release. Why do you have to make everything so serious?"

Not everyone can be like you, she thought. Her brother could do casual. That's all he ever did. But she'd never done casual. She wasn't sure she could.

But as she thought of Austin's husky voice in her ear, the feel of his lips on her skin, his fingers inside of her…

She wanted that again. And again. And maybe one more time in the shower.

She stuck another ball of cookie dough in her mouth and spoke as she chewed. "Don't even know if I'll see him again."

Chad dropped his head and eyed her. "You got off and he didn't?"

She swallowed and nodded.

"Oh, Mars," he laughed. "Trust me. You'll see him again."

She sure hoped so.

Later that night, after Chad passed out on her couch, she lay awake in her darkened bedroom, staring at her ceiling.

She had never dated much. She'd had a couple of long-term boyfriends who were nice and safe and weren't threatened by her ambition. But nice and safe boys didn't hold their hands at her throat. They didn't slip their hands into her panties in a public place—no matter how secluded—and whisper dirty things into her ear.

She shifted under her covers as she began to get aroused just thinking about him.

She'd always had fantasies, but when she suggested them to her first boyfriend, he'd looked alarmed. Like something was wrong with her for wanting him to use a little force when she'd asked for it. She'd been embarrassed and ashamed and hadn't bothered any of her other boyfriends with a similar request.

So her fantasies were for her only. She kept a private Tumblr account and a vibrator and she thought that was all she needed. Of course she longed for the real thing, but worried it could never live up to how she thought it would be.

Until Austin.

She picked up her cell from her nightstand and pulled up her Tumblr app on her phone. She scrolled to her favorites and there it was, that GIF that had started it all.

It had always excited her, this vision of the man controlling the pleasure of this woman. Except now she knew what it actually felt like.

And damn, but the reality was better than the fantasy. So much better. Because Austin had brought to life all her senses—the touch of his hands on her skin and the sound of his voice at her ear and the smell of his scent on her skin.

Now she pictured Austin, those sea-green eyes glowing as he stood behind her. She felt his hand at her throat, the pads of his fingers digging into her skin, the constriction of her air, just enough so she couldn't forget who was in control.

His palm coasting down her stomach. His hand slipping into the front of her thong and dipping between her wet folds.

She moaned softly, and raised her hips, not even realizing her hand had followed the same path and was now inside her panties. Her fingers were a sad substitute for Austin's but she was achy and aroused and she needed to get off.

She closed her eyes and swirled her fingers around her

clit, biting her lip as the orgasm began to build. Quick, so quick. She'd never gotten herself off this fast.

Austin's words. His breath. His hands. That obscene bulge in the front of his pants.

The orgasm ripped through her and she clamped her other hand over her mouth to stifle the sounds.

She flopped her hands back onto the bed, spent, breathing hard. Wishing she could curl herself around a strong male body—Austin.

She picked up her phone and lazily scrolled through her favorites, lingering on a picture of a woman with her back against the wall, blindfolded. A man kneeled in front of her, one of the woman's legs thrown over his shoulder, his face pressed into her.

Despite the fact that she'd just come, Marley found herself staring at the picture.

Trust me, you'll see him again, her brother's words echoed in her head.

She turned her phone off and tossed it on the nightstand.

She sure hoped he was right.

B y Wednesday, she hadn't seen Austin. Which was fine because she was busy in meetings and getting her team organized for the next issue. She didn't have time to daydream about Austin.

Which didn't stop her from zoning out at inappropriate times.

During an unusual lull from work at the end of the day Wednesday, her email pinged. She kept on top of her inbox.

Always had. Because as soon as she let that go, her whole job became harder.

So she clicked over and almost swallowed her tongue when she saw the email was from AricoftheLobby@gmail. com.

It couldn't be anyone but him. Could it?

She opened the email:

FROM: ARICOFTHELOBBY

TO:MARLEYLAKE@GAMERSMAG.COM

ARE YOU WONDERING HOW I TASTE?

—A

She'd never thought she could get wet from six words in plain, Times New Roman font. But as she shifted in her chair, she knew she was. She craved privacy so she could take care of this properly.

Damn him for doing this to her at work. It was so inappropriate, and yet that's what turned her on the most. That everyone around her thought she was some uptight, controlling, frigid woman, not knowing that Saturday night, she'd been fingered in a movie theater lobby.

How was this her life now?

"Marley?"

She jolted at the sound of her name and quickly closed the email. She brushed her hair behind her ear and turned around. "Yes?"

She knew she looked anything but casual by the way Owen eyed her over the rim of his glasses. "You okay?"

She nodded at her second-in-command. "Yes?"

"Are you asking?"

"No?" She couldn't stop raising her voice at the end. She was going to kill Austin when she saw him next. *After* she got that damn taste.

Owen leaned a hip on her desk. "Marley."

She waved a hand and shook herself. "Yes, I'm fine. Just…distracted. Sorry. What's up?"

He ran a finger over the head of her Yoda paperweight. "How was your weekend?"

She smiled. "It was good." Owen was the closest friend she had in the office. At first, she'd sensed that many of the men under her resented working for a woman. Or maybe that was her own paranoia. Owen had never acted like that. Not once. And now her employees treated her with nothing but respect. They still didn't really know her though. Owen's quiet, steady presence melted some of her frost enough to open up to him.

"Yeah? What'd you do?"

"Went to see *Aric's Revenge* with my brother." *And had the best orgasm in my life about fifteen feet away from the popcorn maker.* "How was yours?

He shrugged. "Read that new Connor Takumi mystery."

One of these days, she was going to drag Owen out on a weekend, even if he was kicking and screaming. "Wow, look at you being wild and crazy."

He smiled at her. "Not my thing."

Owen had big, round blue eyes framed with blond lashes. He wore his slicked hair parted to one side. He seemed to do everything he could to blend in, which was a shame, because he was downright adorable. Shy, but adorable.

Like a little nerdy puppy dog.

"So no hot date with some nice librarian in a pencil skirt?" she asked.

His eyes sparkled. "Not my type."

"A librarian?"

He leaned in closer. "A woman."

Oh. Well then. She cocked her head. "I thought my gaydar was better than that."

He tucked a lock of her hair behind her ear and winked.

Her email pinged again and she closed her eyes. When she opened them again, Owen still stared at her. When she didn't respond, he straightened and walked away, shaking his head and chuckling.

Cute, nosy brat.

She turned back to her computer and worried her lip as she read Austin's email again. Then she put her hands on the keyboard.

A ustin sat in his home office, elbow on the arm of his leather chair, and stared at his computer screen.

He didn't know why he was doing this to himself. Why the one woman he couldn't have was the one he wanted with every heartbeat.

He should tell her who he was, that he was technically her boss, but he knew once he did, this would be over. She'd end it—any smart woman would. And Marley wasn't dumb.

He'd avoided the entire industrial complex that week, not wanting to run into Marley and be unable to school his features. Because all he wanted to do was shove her someplace private and get another taste.

But today, his resolve had broken down.

Emailing her was risky, but Austin had taken all precautions that this email wouldn't be seen by anyone. If he couldn't have her physically, then he'd allow himself this, teasing her with filthy words in serif font. Maybe this would be enough, and he could curb the ache for her in his gut. He tried to guess what other fantasies Marley was into. He wasn't sure if it was torture for her but it was pretty much waterboarding to him.

He still couldn't stop himself.

He didn't want a relationship. A relationship meant talking about himself. It meant another person—other than Grant—knowing things about him. He couldn't do that, didn't *want* to do that.

He didn't plan to change, mainly because he didn't date. When the need for physical affection began to claw at his skin, he traveled out of town and met a woman at a bar. He rented a hotel room and that was that. Of course, that sex was almost always very vanilla, which barely took the edge off, but it was better than nothing.

But Marley… Smart, strong, beautiful Marley. He found himself wondering if she could actually like him for himself. Although he wondered if he even knew who that was anymore. What if he opened up to her? Even a little bit?

It was ridiculous that the one woman he was attracted to in such a long time was his employee.

So no, he wouldn't tell her who he was. She didn't need to know, since nothing more would happen. That's what he told himself, anyway. The last person who'd known everything had been his father, and that had gone to shit. In Austin's head, keeping people in their own compartments, on a need-to-know basis, made the most sense.

He felt a tug of guilt at not telling Grant about this. But now there was another tug, like two hooks in his chest. Because he was keeping something from Marley, too. Something that could affect her career—and his—if anyone found out.

Goose bumps pricked his arms as he thought about how he was already breaking so many rules with Marley. The public nature of the hotel lobby. These emails—even if he used a fake account.

His body jolted as a return email hit his inbox.

FROM: MARLEYLAKE@GAMERSMAG.COM
TO: ARICOFTHELOBBY@GMAIL.COM

YES. I'M GUESSING YOU'RE NOT CHERRY FLAVOR.

—M

Austin barked out a laugh. The harsh sound surprised him. When was the last time he laughed like that with a woman about something sexual?

He shifted in his chair as he hardened in his dress pants.

He had wondered if she'd chastise him for emailing her at work. And part of him wondered if she'd realize it was him.

But no, his Marley was playing along. And making him laugh.

The muscles in his face hurt. Maybe he should smile more.

FROM: ARICOFTHELOBBY@GMAIL.COM

To: MarleyLake@gamersmag.com

I don't think I'm as sweet as you.

— A

The return email came half an hour later. A half hour he spent color-coding his pens.

From: MarleyLake@gamersmag.com
To: Aricofthelobby@gmail.com

That's okay. I like savory, too.

— M

He was officially hard. And officially unable to do any work that required more than a single brain cell's worth of concentration.

He pushed away from his desk and stalked out of his office. His facial muscles fell back into his comfortable scowl. He opened up the refrigerator and glared at the contents. Then he slammed the door shut and walked upstairs.

He'd built a house at the end of a quiet street full of older homes and even older residents. His home wasn't visible from the road, as it was built about five hundred yards back in an acre of woods, accessible by a twisty driveway that was a bitch to shovel in the winter. His snow blower was his best friend in January.

When he got to his bedroom, he directed his glare at his empty bed.

He'd already taken a shower that morning, but this hard

on wasn't going away and he needed to surround himself with white noise.

He pulled his tie loose and then unbuttoned his shirt, slipped off his shoes and socks, and stepped out of his pants.

He walked naked into his bathroom, to his large, tiled shower with a showerhead he'd spent way too much money on. He'd grown up in a home with a small water tank and a shower with water pressure so bad, he swore he walked around with a permanent film on his body. So if he wanted to spend hundreds on a showerhead now, he was sure as hell going to do it.

He stepped into the steaming water, not really surprised that his hard on hadn't lessened. Not one bit.

He leaned back against the shower wall and let the water pelt his chest and stomach. He gathered soap in his palm and ran his hand down between his legs, rolling his balls in his fingers. He groaned and closed his eyes, imagining Marley kneeling at his feet, those hazel eyes staring up at him, those full, pink lips wrapped around his cock. He gripped his shaft and began to stroke. His own hand was a poor substitute but imagination was a powerful thing. He imagined Marley's soft moans, his fingers tangled in her thick, wet, curly hair.

"Touch yourself," he whispered to her, and then watched as her hand disappeared between her legs.

Her hips rocked in time with her head as she bobbed on his cock, her cheeks hollowing as she sucked and swirled her tongue around the tip.

He moaned and heard her echo him as she took him deep, so deep that he touched the back of her throat.

He could feel his orgasm building. He widened his legs

and dug his toes into the non-skid shower floor. His balls drew up and he whispered, "Come."

And she did, with a moan that seeped out around his cock in her mouth as she rode her hand to completion. And then Austin was there. Coming and coming down her throat. And then she pulled back and gave him a smirk.

But when he opened his eyes, his cock was half-soft in his hands, his release washing down the drain.

He groaned and turned around, thudding his head on the shower wall. He'd never gotten off like that before, thinking about a specific woman.

And it made him wonder if he would ever get Marley and her playful smirk out of his head.

He slammed his hand down on the faucet of the shower, shutting off the water, and grabbed a towel off the rack. This was crazy. He was crazy. She'd infected his blood like a damn drug and the only way to get rid of the pain was to have her again.

Which wouldn't happen. Nope. Austin was totally in control. Just a little midday shower while fantasizing about her mouth. Completely normal.

He shook himself and finished drying off, then looped the towel around his neck. He padded into his bedroom and perused his walk-in closet. He picked a new shirt and dress pants. He didn't plan to leave the house but he worked more efficiently if he dressed the professional part.

Everything in its compartment.

When he returned to his office, he'd just begun to work, answering emails and other things that didn't require too much concentration, when his phone rang.

He hit the speaker. "Rivers."

"You can't say hello?" Grant's voice came over the line, a smile behind it.

"Ah, and what's the reason for this call, Osprey?" Austin leaned back in his chair.

"So formal."

"So annoying."

Grant grunted. "I have another offer for you."

Austin leaned forward and braced his forearms on his desk. He'd been considering selling his ownership in *Gamers*. *Aric's Revenge* had filled out his savings quite nicely and he'd been looking into simplifying, since they were in the beginning stages of a sequel.

But *Gamers* was one of his first investments. His love. He'd met Grant freshman year of college. They'd both worked shifts at the computer lab in the Math and Science building at Harkton University. It wasn't until a fire drill in their dorm did they realize they lived on the same floor. But computer science majors weren't known for their outgoing personalities. Grant had overcome that shyness. Austin embraced it like a security blanket.

Except when it came to sex. And Marley.

Austin cleared his throat and kept his mind on the conversation. He picked at a scratch in the desk and frowned. "And how does this one sound?"

"Fair."

"You know him or her?"

"Him and yes."

Austin hummed. "And how much?"

"One million, paid in four installments over a year from the date of the contract. Half at signing, the rest in the remaining three payments."

Austin ran his tongue over his teeth. That was the best offer he'd received yet. "Who is it?"

A pause on the other end of the line. Austin almost asked if the call had dropped when Grant's voice came across softly. "Ethan."

Austin held in a growl. Grant's friend, Ethan Talley. "I see."

Grant blew out a breath. "Austin, knock it off with the 'I see.' I know Ethan's not your best buddy, but I like him. He's responsible and reliable and smart."

Austin clenched his jaw. Grant had met Ethan at some conference he'd been to years ago, and Austin wasn't thrilled about it. He recognized that he was a little overprotective of Grant but he'd seen his friend struggle as a new father, as a single dad. So the thought of the magazine—Grant's livelihood—in someone else's hands made Austin nervous. What if they made a bad decision? What if the buyer wasn't trustworthy?

Ethan was smart and business-savvy; Austin knew that. He'd made millions in college as a video game commentator—recording himself playing walkthroughs and posting them to YouTube. His subscriber base was huge, and the revenue from his ads made him millions. It was what he did after that which made Austin nervous. "Ethan—"

"That was a couple of years ago," Grant said softly, cutting him off. "He's changed since then."

Ethan had been driving his sports car with his sister as the passenger, lost control, and wrecked it. The accident killed his sister and permanently scarred Ethan.

"So you think he's a wise choice to own a business with?" Austin asked.

"I considered buying you out myself. I wasn't interested in another partner, someone I didn't know. It was either you or no one. Until Ethan stepped up. Which is nice, because I really didn't want to cough up the extra money."

Austin shifted in his chair. "This is a rather dramatic way to tell me."

Grant laughed. "Ah, but you know us. Everything has to have a flair."

"Yes, yes, I do know you. Ethan, I'm sure, couldn't care less how you told me."

"So you going to think about it and let me know?"

They'd started this magazine together. It'd been Grant's idea over beer and chicken wings. Austin could still picture his young, flushed face as he waved his hands around dramatically. The next morning Austin hadn't been sure if the indigestion was from the food or the plans scribbled on Dale's Pub napkins.

Lately, though, Austin was restless and stretched thin. His brain was screaming at him to simplify.

Getting involved with an employee sure as hell wasn't simplifying. Although, if he sold his share in *Gamers*, she wouldn't be his employee.

He growled under his breath at himself. *Focus.*

"Austin?"

"I might want to speak to Ethan, make sure of his intentions—"

"Good God, Austin, I'm not marrying Sydney off to the man. I trust Ethan to handle the business with me. I do most of the work myself now anyway."

Austin gritted his teeth until his jaw ached. "I'll think about it and let you know. I'm being indecisive about whether I want to sell." *And I don't trust Ethan.*

Grant chuckled. "That's so unlike you."

He knew that, which was why he was irritated. This whole thing was a splinter under his skin. "I realize that."

"You doing okay? You sound…more brusque than usual."

"Brusque?"

"Surly."

"Surly?"

Grant was laughing now. "Terse and crusty."

Austin narrowed his eyes at the phone. "I will accept terse. I absolutely, unequivocally reject crusty."

Grant kept laughing. "Fuck, Austin, never change."

Austin sighed. If those were the words his closest friend used to describe him, didn't that mean a change would be welcome?

"I just wish…" Grant paused. "I wish you would let people in once in a while. I get that what your mom did fucked you up, and what your dad did fucked you over, but if you keep going down this path, you're going to end up exactly like him."

"Oh yeah?" Austin snapped. "And how's that? Because he's six feet below now."

"Alone." Grant didn't back down. "He shut everyone out. He was alone before he died, and he's buried in a plot all by himself. Is that what you want?"

A couple of years ago, he might have said yes. But lately…well, he wasn't so sure.

"Well, I appreciate your opinion, Grant. I'll be in touch."

"Aus—"

He hung up the phone. And then thumped his forehead

on the desk. Being reminded of his mom and dad, well, that always threw him for a loop and soured his mood. Austin had never actually met his mother—she'd left them shortly after he was born. His father was…cold. He worked a lot and when he was home, he didn't have much time for the son he was left with. Austin learned quickly that he couldn't rely on his father for much of anything. He cooked for himself, cleaned up after himself, and worked his ass off at school. If he could make the grades, earn a scholarship, he'd be able to support himself, wouldn't have to rely on anyone ever again.

So when Austin was successful, and his father—whom Austin had trusted despite everything—stole money from him, it was the last time he allowed himself to trust anyone.

He closed ranks, retreated into his shell. And that's where he stayed. He didn't want to trust anyone because that way no one could betray him.

Grant was somewhat of an anomaly, mainly because he had a way of barreling into Austin's life without him even realizing it. Although, that's why he cared about his friend so much. Grant was one of a kind.

Which was why he had to make sure Grant was making the right decision, and that he was placing his trust in the right business partner.

Austin would be sure of that before he sold anything.

Chapter Five

Marley crossed her legs and stared at the email.

From: Aricofthelobby@gmail.com
To: MarleyLake@gamermag.com

I think my red silk tie would look best around the skin of your wrists as I touch every inch of you with my tongue.

—A

It was Friday and he'd tortured her all damn week with these emails. It was like he'd found her Tumblr account and placed himself and her in every one of those pictures or GIFs. To say it turned her on would be an understatement.

Hell, he probably did find her Tumblr account. All those guys had hacker skills, didn't they?

Oh Lord.

She licked her lips and after a glance around the almost empty office, placed her hands on the keyboard. She thought of that GIF, the blindfolded woman, and the man on his knees in front of her.

FROM: MARLEYLAKE@GAMERSMAG.COM
TO: ARICOFTHELOBBY@GMAIL.COM

WHAT COLOR WOULD LOOK BEST ON MY FACE WHEN YOU BLINDFOLD ME?

— M

She giggled to herself. That man needed a taste of his own medicine.

"What's so funny?"

She nearly jumped out of her skin at the sound of Owen's voice. She braced a hand on her chest in a lame attempt to slow her racing heart and turned to glare at him. "Do you have to sneak up on me? We need to get you a damn cat collar with a bell, you little ninja."

He jingled his pockets, which she assumed held his keys or some loose change. "You want me to always announce my presence by doing this?"

She haughtily stuck her nose in the air. "Yes, and shout 'Marco' or something."

He snorted. "So, Polo, you hear the news?"

"What news?"

"Bradley's leaving."

She jerked her head back at the thought of their assistant editor leaving. "Really?" She liked the guy, although he wasn't hands-on enough as a leader in her opinion. Still, he let her run her team the way she liked and for that, she was grateful.

Owen nodded, his round blue eyes flitting to the door of Bradley's office and then back to her. "Rumor is they're looking to hire within to replace him."

Marley sat up straighter. Bradley's job was everything she dreamed of. Her fingers in all the pies of *Gamers*. Organizing them. Leading them. Of course, that bastard Jack would want it, too.

Her nemesis.

Owen knew she wanted this job, because a smile crept across his face. "I figured you'd want to know about this."

"How'd you find out?"

"He let it slip when we were talking about the spring releases. He's announcing it at the end of the week."

She needed to focus. Get herself and her libido under control and her eyes on the prize. "I want that damn job."

Owen laughed. "I know, Marley."

She reached out and gripped his tie. "Tell me all of the vital information."

He tugged his tie out of her grip. "That's all I know, KGB. Calm down."

She growled under her breath. "You better not be holding out on me."

He winked. "Wouldn't dream of it."

She turned around and concentrated on her work.

"Hey, Polo!" Owen called.

She rolled her eyes before turning to him. "Yes, Marco?"

"I'm heading out. You okay? The night cleaning crew should be by in a bit."

Marley looked around the office. "Am I the last one

here?" *Again?*

Owen looked around. "Might be one or two stragglers."

Marley waved him off. "It's cool. I'll be fine. Going to finish some stuff and get set up for Monday and them I'm outtie."

He waved as he walked toward the door. "Have a good weekend."

"You too!" she called after him.

Marley finished the second round of copy edits on an article about a controller redesign and then wrote the headline. She straightened her desk and tossed out her three candy bar wrappers, vowing to bring something healthy next week, like granola.

While shutting down her computer, she remembered that her mouse had been acting up. Knowing they had ordered some new ones last month, she headed to the supply closet. She wanted to get one plugged in and installed so she wouldn't have to deal with it Monday.

She walked down the narrow hallway by the bathrooms at the back of the office and flashed her keycard in front of the sensor. The door shut behind her as she perused the shelves and filing cabinets for the new computer parts. She was running her fingers over the plastic wrapped keyboards when there was a beep from the door behind her, signaling someone else was coming in.

She figured it was the cleaning crew. "Be done in a minute," she said, bending to reach back for a new black mouse.

No sound came from behind her and, clutching the mouse, she straightened and turned to see who'd entered.

It wasn't a janitor or any member of the cleaning crew. Marley's body locked as she met those amazing sea-green eyes she hadn't seen for a week. At least, not in person, be-cause she sure as hell saw them in her dreams.

Austin stood with his back to the door, hair slightly askew like he'd been running his fingers through it. Suit pants clung to his long legs, accentuating his narrow hips, and his white shirt was unbuttoned at the top, revealing a tantalizing amount of smooth, tan skin.

And wrapped around his fist was a pale blue tie, one end dangling almost to the ground.

His lips were parted, his broad shoulders not moving. Instead his breath was only visible in the slow rise and fall of his chest. He was the picture of control except for his hair and wild eyes. And she was turned on all over again.

"Austin." Her eyes darted to the doorknob sensor under his arm, but the light was a steady red. The office was nearly empty, but this was still risky. And how did he have a key for the door? IT must have it for supplies.

When his voice came, it was soft, yet firm. "I liked you better as you were."

He had a way of speaking that seemed to switch off her brain so her body went on autopilot. Which she needed, because if she thought about this too much, she'd stop him. She'd brush past him and walk out that door to preserve her sanity and her job.

His words hadn't even been a command, yet she could do nothing but turn around, presenting her back to him, bending slightly at the hip so that her ass stuck out. An invi-tation. A present.

After agonizing minutes passed, or maybe it was only a few seconds, the click of his shoes on the linoleum came closer, and she hoped he planned to unwrap her. She bit her lip as the steps stopped behind her. And she waited.

The first touch was against her backside, just a brush of the front of his pants so that she could feel he was hard. Then a hand gripped her shoulders, his thumb at the knob at the top of her spine, his other fingers digging into her muscle. Lips ran along the shell of her ear.

"Do you want to know the answer to the question in your email?"

Heat radiated from his body, warming her back, yet a shiver ran down her body. Goosebumps popped out on her arms. What was the question he asked? Fuck, she couldn't think with those fingers gripping her, that hardness caressing the crease of her ass through her skirt.

"I…" Her voice tapered off into a moan as those lips sucked on the skin behind her ear. But he didn't just suck. He licked and nipped that small area of skin until she swore she would come from that alone, from the blood rushing to the surface.

He pulled back and she gasped.

"You asked what color blindfold would look good, didn't you?"

Her mouth worked but her throat didn't. So she nodded.

Austin held the blue tie up to her eyes. "I selected this just for you." He was grinding into her now with small rolls of his hips. She wanted that hot length in her hand. In her mouth. Anywhere.

"I tried not to think about you, Marley. But I can't stop hearing your little moans. I can't stop feeling your wetness on my hand. And I can't stop tasting you on my tongue."

The tie slipped over her eyes, and she closed her lids as he tied it at the back of her head.

His voice was already sharper, his touch more sensational. "What other fantasies are you keeping to yourself, Evelyn?"

She arched her back more, pleased with the nickname from the video game. "Austin."

A smack rent the air, and a painful heat bloomed across her left ass cheek.

"Don't move." That voice. Not harsh, but so much authority behind it. "Maybe I'll just have to try a couple of things. You tell me when I root out a fantasy, okay?"

He'd already hit one. The slight dip in his voice let her know he knew it, too. She wiggled her hips slightly, and got another crack on the ass for it. She smiled. "Then get on with it, my Aric of the lobby."

Silence. Then both hands gripped her waist, and he shoved her forward into the shelves in front of her. His breath puffed in her ear, like an abbreviated chuckle. "You liked the emails."

"Yes." She paused. "But aren't our accounts monitored?"

"I took care of that," he murmured, pushing her mass of hair over one shoulder, lips skimming the back of her neck. Then they stopped. "Do you trust me?"

Yes. That was crazy though, right? She didn't know him. She didn't even know his last name. But yet, she did trust him. In the lobby of the movie theater, she always felt like she could have said "no," or "stop," and he would have. He had a way of silently asking permission without losing the thrill of this type of sex.

She'd allowed herself to be locked in a supply closet with this guy, blindfolded, with his hard cock grinding into her ass.

That either meant she trusted him or she was crazy.

She was going to go with trust.

"What's your last name?" she asked, instead of answering his question.

Those lips, which had resumed mapping of the top of her back above her thin tank top, stopped. "Rivers."

She laughed. "Lake and Rivers? There's a joke there, but I'm too turned on to think of it."

"We're drowning in each other." She could hear the smile in his voice.

"So cheesy."

He cleared his throat. "Is that a river in your panties or are you just happy to see me?"

Her roar of laughter was loud in the confined space. "My Aric of the lobby is funny. Who knew?"

There was a pause. "I sure didn't." His voice held a tinge of sadness, but before she could think more about it, a hand wrapped around her neck at the base of her throat. "What you do to me, Marley Lake." That husky voice was back in her ear, thumb caressing the cord on the side of her neck.

Then his other hand pulled down a strap of her tank top, so it hung loosely at her elbow. He pressed a kiss to her shoulder then skimmed his fingers along the top of her breast. "You even have freckles here." His touch moved back and forth in an arch on her skin, tracing the swell of her breast and then dipping into her cleavage. He pulled down the cup of her bra, the lace on the edge catching on her hard nipple. She bit her lip, waiting for him to torture that aching nub, but instead she felt a tug on her lower lip.

She opened her mouth and he slipped in two fingers. She closed her lips around the digits and swirled her tongue, licking and sucking. She imagined the picture she made, light blue tie over her eyes, his fingers in her mouth. But she didn't care, because she wanted those fingers back where they'd been in the movie theater lobby. She wanted him to make her fly, like no one before him had ever done.

He pulled out his fingers, and seconds later, her nipple was pulled with a slick pinch. He ran a finger around the areola, flicking the nipple with a blunt fingernail, then rolling it.

Her breath escaped her lips in gasps as he continued the delicious torture.

In a quick maneuver, she was turned, her back pressed against the wall, a shock of cool in contrast to the hot male body that had previously blanketed her. But she didn't have time to contemplate it, because her nipple was now encased in wet heat and teeth were abrading the sensitive skin around it.

His lips left her and then fabric slipped over her arm, letting her know he'd lowered the remaining strap of her tank top. Cool air hit her other nipple as he pulled down her bra.

For a moment, all she felt was his hand at the base of her throat, his thumb caressing the skin.

A click and the front clasp of her bra popped open. Another tug and her tank top pooled above the waistband of her skirt.

She wished she could see his face as he looked his fill. Would those sea-green eyes swirl with lust? Would they darken with arousal? Was he deciding what to do next, or was this moment of pause on purpose?

"So beautiful," he whispered.

Marley rubbed her legs together, wanting, needing friction, and received a solid slap on the hip for it. She yelped and then laughed.

His breath rushed over her cheek. "Is this a game to

you?"

She knew he physically hid his emotions well. But blindfolded, she clung to his voice, feeling out the words and letting them roll around in her head until an emotion seeped out of the seams.

This time, there was slight vulnerability.

She shook her head. "Not a game, but…when I'm enjoying something, I smile and laugh and make jokes. Don't you?"

Another pause. "Not usually. But with you…" He let his voice trail off, reverence tainting the words.

She took a chance, hoping her question wouldn't end this moment. "Is there anyone else?"

His hand at her throat squeezed and then relaxed. "No, and there hasn't been for some time."

She swallowed. "Same with me."

A puff of breath on her lips. "I realized…I forgot something when I came in."

"A red tie for my wrists?"

A small chuckle. "No, this." And then he kissed her, instantly invading, plundering, conquering, and she let him, her Aric of the lobby. She braced her hands on the cool cinder block wall behind her and let him guide her jaw with slight pressure from his thumb. Because, as of now, she trusted that she was his only Evelyn.

He eased back with small nips to her lips, down her jaw, and back to her ear. He ran his fingers along the inside of her thigh and she held her breath, waiting until he reached the top of her thigh-high stockings.

A strangled sound rumbled from his throat when he did, and those fingers caressed where the lace met her bare skin, over and over again, like he enjoyed the boundary.

"Oh, Marley," he breathed. "Have you ever orgasmed from cunnilingus before?"

She almost orgasmed by the end of that sentence. Cunnilingus. She'd never thought that word was sexy. It was medical and Latin. But the way Austin said it? In that husky voice, his hot breath at her ear, his fingers tracing tantalizing patterns on the inside of her thigh? God, she wanted all the *cun,* and all the *ill,* and all the *lingus* he had to offer.

"Have you?" he asked again.

She couldn't speak above a whisper. "Yes, but it took a long time and…the aid of fingers or something battery-powered."

Those fingers rose, running along the edge of her panty-line. "Ah, so you haven't from me. We will remedy that."

She couldn't speak. Not when his body brushed along the front of hers, not when his tongue dipped into her belly button. Not when he rucked her skirt up to her waist and pulled down her panties, helping her step out of them.

Not when he ordered her to spread, and then took her left leg and hooked it over his shoulder.

Because she was completely open and exposed now, her nipples surely red and shiny from his torment, not to mention her…

"Gorgeous, Marley," he breathed, and she finally made a sound, something that wasn't human. He continued to talk, those damn fingers still caressing her thighs. "Your clit is swollen and so wet. So fucking wet for me, Marley. And I barely touched you."

Oh, he'd touched her a lot, just not with his fingers. It was that damn voice of his, which entered her like a drug. She soaked it up through her pores and now she was addicted. "Please," she whispered.

"Please what?" There was a hint of a smile and she wanted to smack him.

"Please touch me." Impatience threaded through her voice. But she didn't care because she ached so fucking bad for this man and his touch.

He hummed, just a sound that made her think he was going to wait longer, until those humming lips landed right on her clit.

She shouted at the vibration on the sensitive nerves and gripped his hair to steady herself.

He pulled off immediately, and she growled.

"One hand on the wall, the other on my shoulder."

She released her hold on his hair and clutched his shoulder, spreading the fingers of her other hand on the peeling cinder block wall behind her. "Okay."

"Good girl."

This time, she didn't get the hum. He opened her up with his thumbs and thoroughly, possessively, drove her insane.

He licked with the flat of his tongue, then he moved higher to her clit, sucking, swirling. When she thought she would come, he moved back to work her opening with his tongue.

Over and over again, he brought her to the brink and then pulled back. Sounds echoed off the walls of the tiny room, moans and sobs and curses, all from a feminine voice she'd never heard before. It was the sound of a woman coming apart at the seams. And she didn't want it to end.

When he finally let her come, it was with the command, "Fly for me." And fly she did, as he swirled her clit on the tip of his tongue.

Her whole body pulsed as she clutched his shoulder, braced herself on the wall, and ground onto his mouth. He took care of her, licking everything she gave and then holding her as she came down.

Her legs trembled, and her throat hurt. The tie over her eyes was heavy, cold, and sodden. She raised a shaky hand and fingered her cheeks. They came away wet. He'd orgasmed her to tears. That was surely a first.

The sound of a belt buckle, zipper, and then the blindfold was removed.

Marley blinked, but Austin positioned his head so he blocked out the harsh light from the naked bulb on the ceiling. All she saw were his beautiful eyes, his flushed face, and swollen lips.

She flicked her gaze down to the bulge in his pants that had to be almost painful. Then she met his gaze. "Take me."

A small quirk of his lips. "I intend to."

Chapter Six

Austin had resisted placing a condom in his wallet all week. Knowing it was there, he'd feel it, always be aware of it, like a burning brand on his ass.

He'd been fighting the pull of her and he'd been doing a damn good job of it. But that email. *That email.* It'd sent him over the edge. He'd been in his bedroom when he got it. And his gaze had settled on the blue silk tie. So he'd grabbed that and a condom and left.

And now, with Marley satiated and naked in front of him, he thanked everything holy he had broken down. Because this? Well, this was risky as hell. But he couldn't summon any fucks to give. He was fulfilling a fantasy of hers and it just so happened to be one of his. Two adults giving their bodies freely to each other. What was the harm in that? This was all it had to be.

Marley was beautiful and tasted like a dream. She responded to him with everything she had, and most of all?

She made him laugh. She made him want to be funny. He wasn't the guy with lots of smiles and witty jokes. He was Austin, king of taking life too seriously. He knew that, but he didn't know how else to be.

Marley though… She enjoyed life, didn't she?

Take some lessons, pal, said the voice in his head, as he ripped open the condom wrapper with his teeth.

Marley watched him, those hazel eyes steady on his mouth.

After he slid the condom over his length, he reached down and gripped the back of her thighs. Her skin was hot under his palms and her chest rose and fell with deep breaths. Those full breasts topped with rosy pink nipples called to him and he dipped his head, flicking one with his tongue.

"Austin," she moaned.

He moved to the other nipple and nipped it. Her body jolted.

"Yeah?" He pressed a kiss to her breastbone.

Her mouth was slack, but turned up ever so slightly into a small smirk in the corners. "You better get on with it. I owe you three now."

He dug his fingers into her soft thighs, lifted her up, and entered her with one powerful thrust as she wrapped her legs around his waist.

He moaned against her neck and then opened his mouth, setting his teeth into the skin at the top of her shoulder. He couldn't move yet, not when the tight heat of Marley squeezed him, causing all the blood to rush south. He was dizzy and light-headed and wasn't sure how he stayed on his feet. All those times he'd emptied himself in the shower or between his sheets, thinking of her, didn't compare to the reality of sinking into her body.

She swirled her hips and he let out another groan. "You going to fuck me?" she asked breathlessly.

He smiled against her skin, then pulled back. He wrapped his hands around her wrists and slammed them into the wall beside her head. Her mouth fell open and she arched her back, causing him to sink in deeper. "I decide when to move. If I want to stand here with my cock in you while you writhe on it, I'll do that. You understand?"

Even through the condom, he could feel her inner muscles clench at his words. "Yes, Austin."

He slid his hands higher and twined their fingers. "I like the way you say my name." She always drew out the first syllable, almost on a moan. It made his dick twitch.

"Auuuss-tin."

With that, he drew his hips back, pulling out to the tip, and then slammed back into her. She cried out and her fingers flinched in his. Her eyes blazed, and his mission was to make her come again.

He widened his legs and began to thrust into her, each drag a delicious pull of friction on his aching cock.

Because this was Marley. He still bore the taste of her on his tongue, and the tips of her breasts brushed his shirt as they bounced with each jolt. Her entire body was a beautiful pink flush of arousal.

His rhythm stuttered as his balls drew up into his body. The orgasm threatened at the base of his spine and he gritted his teeth to hold it back.

"Come," he ordered her as her head thrashed, her sweat-damp curls brushing his cheek. She was pushing back now, riding his cock with erratic rolls of her hips, chasing her own orgasm.

He changed his angle and pumped harder. "Come, now, my Evelyn. Come."

Her stomach contracted, her eyes squeezed shut, and then she gasped, soft whimpering moans and soft "Oh's". Her inner muscles clamped down and he came with her, unable to hold back as she milked him from the inside.

His release shot through him like a lightning bolt, echoing in all of his limbs. He pressed his forehead to her temple and gasped against her cheek, as he pulsed inside of her.

He was spent. Drained. Finished.

He let go of her hands and she dropped them to her sides. He used the last of his strength to rub the muscles of her shoulders, knowing they were probably sore.

He couldn't look at her, not while he was this raw and exposed and vulnerable.

Not while he was still inside her and still half-hard.

God, he wanted her again already.

He pulled out slowly and helped Marley back to the ground. She wobbled slightly and grabbed the wall behind her.

He pulled off the condom, tied it, and hid it under some papers in a trashcan in the corner.

Marley's eyes were glassy and she looked thoroughly ravished—wild, sweaty hair framing her face, skirt pushed up to her waist, tank top pushed down below her breasts.

Without a word, he put her back together while she watched him with steady eyes and heaving breaths. He clipped her bra, then slipped her arms through her tank top and covered her. He tugged down on her skirt and smoothed it into place.

She deserved to be taken care of. God, she deserved everything for giving him what she had. Herself.

Her trust.

As he tucked himself into his pants and zipped up, he spotted the light blue tie on the floor at his feet. He picked it up and ran his fingers over the fabric, touching the areas where her tears had stained it.

He gripped her wrist and held her hand, palm up. He coiled the length of the tie in her hand and wrapped her fingers around it. "You can keep this," he said.

Now that the rush to orgasm, the rush to be with her had worn off, he realized where they were. A supply closet. At Marley's job. In a building he owned.

For a man who claimed so much control, did he really have any at all?

He met Marley's gaze, wondering if she regretted this. What had he been thinking? Their first time shouldn't have been against a cinder block wall surrounded by computer parts.

First time.

Would there be another? If there wasn't, he might lose his mind.

He opened his mouth, to say what, he wasn't sure. To apologize for taking her in a supply closet? For not asking her out like a proper man?

For not telling her he was—

A beep sounded behind them. Austin moved away from her and stood against the wall by the door.

Marley's eyes widened as the door opened into the room, covering Austin in shadow.

He couldn't see who it was, but Marley recovered quickly,

giving whoever had stepped into the closet a bright smile.

"Oh sorry!" said a male voice. "Didn't know anyone was still here."

"It's okay." Marley reached for something on the shelf near her and then held it up. "Just needed to get a mouse."

"Okay, I was going to tidy up in here. I'll just work on the bathrooms first and pop back in here later."

"That's fine." Marley smiled again, and Austin thought she'd make a great actress. He couldn't believe she looked so put together after what they did.

The door closed, and Austin stepped forward. "Marley, I—"

The smile fell from her face and she held up a trembling hand. "I don't want to regret what we just did, but we almost got caught having sex in the supply closet where we work. That's not okay, Austin. This is so far from professional, I don't even know where to start. You're my *coworker*."

This issue hung like a cloud over them, ready to unleash the rain. He could come clean here, tell her who he was. But Austin couldn't seem to thaw his tongue enough to spill the truth. It wasn't that he didn't think she was trustworthy, it was that he didn't *want* to find her trustworthy. Because as soon as he did, he'd be in deep shit. Deeper than he already was.

Standing there, she looked so fragile. The room smelled like sex. He could still taste her on his tongue.

He'd email her later, maybe, when they weren't both so raw from what happened. This would be it then. The last time he'd have her like this.

So he took a deep breath and said, "You're right."

That brought a larger, much more threatening cloud

over his head, which pulsed with electricity, ready to strike him with lightning at any moment. Because he'd just omitted a hell of a lot by agreeing with her.

Marley shook her head. "I don't know what we were thinking. And I'm not blaming you, because I participated. But this is my job." She stamped her foot on the last word and then pointed a finger at him. "And I know that technically this isn't breaking any company rules, but I can't afford for my coworkers to find out anything that would make them question my performance." She took a shaky breath and gestured between them and then around the room. "I can't do this. You make me…forget myself."

He got that. This was reckless. And ironic, in that he would tell Grant to fire any employees caught having sex in the office. His face burned. "Is that good or bad that I make you forget yourself?"

She bit her lip and eyed him. Then she took a step forward, the tie dangling in her hand. "It's good. It's so incredibly good. And that's why it's bad."

He cupped her cheek and she leaned into it, closing her eyes for a moment. "This job is everything to me. I worked so hard to get where I am. My team respects me and my boss respects me. And I'm applying for a big promotion. I can't let anything get in the way of that. I can't let them find a reason to not give it to me."

He rubbed his thumb along her cheekbone. "You work hard."

She nodded. "I do. I work really hard. And I love my job."

He lowered his hand and tugged her waist so she stepped closer. He wanted to feel her against his body again. He needed it like air, especially knowing this would be it. He'd cut himself off, cold turkey. He could already feel the phantom withdrawals. "What do you love most about your job?"

She smiled and ran her finger over a button on his shirt. "Well, I love video games. Been playing since I got my first game system—A Nintendo SNES—when I was a little girl. My brother and I used to play Mario Brothers."

He nodded because he remembered it. His dad couldn't afford a Nintendo but he'd played at friend's houses.

"And," she continued. "I love helping consumers. Sorting out which game is best. We receive emails all the time from kids who save every penny they make mowing lawns. At the end of the summer, they can afford one game, and our magazine helps them choose."

Austin huffed out a breath. He'd been one of those kids who mowed lawns.

"The assistant editor is leaving and I have a chance to take his place." She lowered her voice to a whisper. "I want it. I want that job so badly, I can taste it."

Austin hadn't known Bradley was leaving. This was even worse than she knew. Because now if anyone found out about them, Marley could be accused of using alternative means to get the job and Austin could be sued for sexual harassment.

Fuck.

Marley wasn't staying in that neat little compartment he'd placed her in. He found his control slipping around her, with every touch of her hand, every laugh that echoed in his ears. He'd come there with the intention of fulfilling her fantasies as well as his own, and he ended up becoming enraptured by her. Her beauty and ambition. Her strength in putting all her trust in him when he touched her. God, what would it feel like to trust someone that much?

She made him want… She made him want more.

And that was how he knew he had to stay away from her, because he was having trouble detaching. Normally, he was able to maintain a distance during sex, so that afterward, leaving was only a matter of buttoning his shirt.

With Marley, he wanted to drag her back home and spend all day in bed, hearing that laugh and feeling that smooth skin beneath his palms. He wanted to wring those whimpers from her until she was hoarse.

And hearing her talk about her career… Well, it made him admire her even more, and also cemented his decision to let her go. This wasn't just about him. This was also about her. He would never forgive himself if he messed up the career that she so loved.

As if her mind was heading down the same path—although with much less information—she took one step back, her hand slipping from his chest. Another step and they were no longer connected. No part of her touched him. All he felt was cool air. And he hated it. The loss of her hands on him was like a limb had been cut off. How had she gotten so far under his skin in such a short amount of time?

She stood in front of him now, beautiful, vibrant, and so damn ambitious. He needed to get away from her before he ruined her life.

He licked his lips and took a deep breath, rolling his shoulders, feeling his armor slip over his skin. Except now it was ill-fitting and he could feel every chink—each one caused by Marley.

He ignored the sensation and focused on her. "You're

right. This was risky, and I'm sorry for putting you in this position." God, it hurt, every word leaving his mouth left cuts along the way. He expected to taste the blood any minute. "I won't bother you again."

He didn't look at her face, just in case she was as weak for him as he was for her. He walked past her, opened the door to the supply closet, and then slipped down the hallway to the back door.

The soles of his dress shoes clacked on the pavement in the parking lot, each footstep echoing off the brick wall as he made his way to his car.

When he reached his car, he did taste the blood, that iron tang. He realized he'd been biting his cheek that hard, the pain not even registering through his foggy brain.

He wanted to sleep for about five years. But he knew he'd dream of Marley.

He slipped behind the wheel of his Jag and slammed his head on the headrest, closing his eyes. He saw Marley behind his lids, her flushed face, wet nipples, aroused pussy.

Well, fuck.

He turned on the ignition and placed his hands on the steering wheel. Then he pulled out of the parking lot, preparing himself for a sleepless night in his lonely, empty house.

Chapter Seven

Marley kept her gaze on her computer screen, but she could see the hallway leading to the supply closet out of the corner of her eye.

And it was driving her crazy.

Two days ago, she'd had the best sex of her life, and then she'd turned it all down for her job. Why had she done that again? Oh, right, because it was a distraction.

As if she wasn't still distracted. Stupid hallway.

She blew out a breath and took another sip of her coffee.

The office had been in a dither all day. Grant Osprey, the owner of *Gamers*, had dropped in, which wasn't necessarily rare, but it was cause for office chatter. He often worked from home, but with the news that Bradley was leaving, any hint of his presence started the rumor mill.

She'd already expressed her interest in the position to the editor in chief, James Mathers. But Grant would sign off on any new hire. She'd never talked to him much, but he'd sat in on her initial interview and asked a few questions.

Her phone rang at her desk.

"Gamers, this is Marley Lake."

"Marley," James's craggy voice said in the line. The man smoked too much. "Do you have a minute to come in to my office?"

"Yep, I'll be right there."

She hung up the phone and glanced down the hallway for the fiftieth time that day. Okay, that hour.

Dammit.

She stood up and smoothed her skirt, checking for any runs in her nylons. She slipped her feet into her heels and walked in the direction of James's office.

She knocked on the door and then turned the knob after she heard a curt, "Come in."

She smiled at James, but that smile faltered when she caught sight of Grant in the room, sitting across from James's desk, his posture sprawled, one hand propped on the arm of his chair.

He straightened as she walked in, and then stood up with his hand out. "How's it going, Marley?"

She shook his hand and sat down when he gestured to the seat beside him. They both sat as James watched from behind his desk. "Good, Grant, and you?"

He shrugged. "Can't complain."

She'd always found Grant attractive. He was kind of like a Ken doll, tall and fit, with golden hair and blue eyes. He was usually smiling, but he seemed a little unfocused to her, like he existed with his head in the clouds. Being around him a lot would drive her crazy, she was sure.

She liked someone calmer, more focused and controlled.

Like Austin.

Stop it, she admonished herself.

She crossed her legs and faced the desk. "Hello, James."

He grunted a greeting. "We're scheduling interviews for the assistant editor position."

That perked Marley's ears. She straightened her spine and nodded.

"Grant wants to sit it on them, as usual, so we're trying to coordinate schedules. How about the eighteenth?"

That was about three weeks away, which gave her plenty of time to prepare and beef up her résumé. "Sure, what time?"

James deferred to Grant, who tapped his temple. "Two in the afternoon."

"That okay with you?" James asked her.

She nodded. "Perfect."

James clasped his hands on his desk. "What we're looking for is leadership skills, time management, and professionalism."

So, not screwing the IT guy in the closet, she thought.

James continued. "You've shown those skills in your current position, but the managing editor job is a lot more work. So if you can present some ways you'd handle it differently and improve the efficiency of *Gamers,* we'd love to hear it."

Mission accepted. "I can do that. Thanks again for the opportunity to apply for this position."

James knocked on his desk. "Of course. You know you're one of my favorite employees."

She hadn't known that, but she appreciated it. "Thanks, James."

He smiled. "You're free to get back to work now."

She turned to Grant and murmured her good-byes, then walked back to her desk. She had to stay focused. This was her job, her career.

She sat down at her computer and edited one column before her gaze drifted back to that damn hallway.

This didn't bode well for her concentration.

"So let me get this straight." Chad threw a handful of popcorn into this mouth and faced her on the couch. "You sent each other explicit emails for about a week, then he clicked your mouse in a supply closet, and then you two decided to never see each other again."

"I can't believe you just said that." Marley banged the TV remote against her thigh. Damn thing was finicky.

"Oh, yeah, I split my infinite. Sorry about that."

Marley glared at him as he smirked. "The tech puns are getting old."

"You rode his joystick."

"Not again—"

"He uploaded his data to your motherboard."

"Seriously, you need to stop."

Chad pouted. "Please get married, because I will make a bangin' best man speech."

"Who says you'll be invited?"

He gasped in mock outrage. "Shut your mouth!"

Marley sighed. "Come on, Chad. I want to forget about my failed hookup with the sexiest man of my dreams, okay? I sacrificed him for my job and right now, I'm starting to second-guess myself, so can we kindly not talk about it?"

His face softened. "I'm sorry, Mars."

"Yeah, me too."

They watched a movie, a super sad depressing one that didn't end in a happily ever after for the couple because Marley said she wanted to feel why love hurts. But in the end, it only made her sadder, as she sobbed into her tissues as the woman threw flowers onto the grave of her lover.

Marley kicked Chad out afterward, even though he'd offered to stay, alarmed by her blotchy face and leaking eyes. But she wanted to be alone with her cat. Which made her even more depressed because how pathetic was she, crying over a sad movie with her cat? Grade A pathetic.

She walked into the small office in her apartment and gazed at the plaques on the wall as Sadie rubbed her ankles. She'd graduated summa cum laude from Penn State with a bachelor's in journalism, then went on to graduate school for a master's in media studies. She'd worked at her local newspaper for years, first as a beat reporter, then moving on to specialized technology reporter for the arts and entertainment section. She'd always loved video games and that was where she had started her regular gaming column. From there, she'd accepted a position at *Gamers* and had been with the magazine ever since.

Her diplomas hung on the wall, representing years of her life spent in class and pulling all-nighters to write papers or cram for tests. She'd been so set on her grades and studies, she hadn't been the type of student that let go. Even now, she listened to coworkers tell stories about drunken college nights, and she laughed and pretended she knew what they were talking about.

She didn't, of course, because she'd been holed up in the

computer lab or hard at work proofing pages on deadline for the campus newspaper.

So many years. So much control.

Which was why, in Austin's arms, she could breathe. Interesting that it took a hand around her throat and a tie over her eyes for her to feel alive.

She wasn't ashamed that that was what she needed in the bedroom, er, supply closet. But she sure as hell hadn't trusted anyone before Austin. The fact that she did trust him was crazy, but she did. His presence alone was soothing, just the sound of his voice enough to make her feel like her puppet strings—which she pulled herself—had finally been cut.

It had felt so good to let her limbs turn to jelly and her brain to mush in his arms.

Marley groaned and plopped down on the floor, slapping her palm onto her forehead. She'd come in here to remind herself why she cared so much about her job. Why she was fighting so hard to forget about Austin and move up in the ranks at work.

But all she did was think more about Austin. After the supply closet mishap, which was a total lapse in judgment, she'd told herself he was too close to her job. There was no rule or company policy that she couldn't see him, so it was more her own policy that, at the time, she'd thought was important.

But the more she thought about it, the more irritated she became that the hypothetical opinions of her coworkers were what kept her back. As long as she didn't do anything stupid like get locked in a supply closet with him again, she could handle this, couldn't she?

Didn't she deserve a life outside of *Gamers*?

A meow made Marley open her eyes. Sadie was nudging her wrist, begging for some head scratches. Marley obliged. "What am I gonna do about that man, Sadie?" Marley crooned, not letting herself dwell on the fact that she'd sunk so low that she was talking to her cat about her sex life.

Sadie meowed again and arched her back. Marley moved her hand to scratch the base of her tail. "Do you think we could see each other in secret?"

Another meow.

"Is that a yes or no?"

Sadie blinked at her.

"Okay," Marley crossed her legs and held up her hands. "We're going to vote." Marley held out both of her hands, palms up, on her knees. "So, this is up to you. If you want scratches from my right hand, then I'll call Austin. If you want scratches from my left hand, I'll go get B.O.B. and try to forget Austin exists." Then she waited. Austin had made it rather clear the ball was in her court. It was her job on the line. It was she who was up for promotion.

She wiggled her fingers at a purring Sadie, who sat in front of Marley on her haunches. "Well? Which one?"

Sadie stared at her, then turned up her nose and walked out of the room.

Marley threw her hands up in the air. "Are you kidding me!" she yelled as her cat's tail disappeared around the doorframe. "Thanks a lot, you dumb cat!"

Marley stared at her hands, now flat on her thighs. Why did life have to be so complicated?

The ant ran in figure eights along the wrinkled edge of the blanket. Austin watched it weave back and forth, then up his thumb and over the back of his hand, pausing at a vein before making its descent back onto the blanket.

The erratic movement made him twitch.

Austin leaned back on his hands and crossed his jean-clad legs at the ankle, wiggling his bare toes. A slight breeze ruffled the colored leaves above them and a few fell onto the ground in front of him, one red and one orange.

Sydney sat cross-legged beside him on the blanket, crunching a handful of chips. Once a month, he took her to the park for a picnic. He'd been doing it since he and Grant had graduated college. Austin wanted to help out his friend, so he offered to take her out, although back then, they'd spent all the time on the playground. Now, they relaxed in the shade of a tree and ate food from the deli that wasn't particularly healthy.

Sometimes he wondered when he'd arrive to pick her up and find out she'd preferred to go on a date with a boyfriend or go see a movie with friends.

But so far, that hadn't happened. She answered the door with a smile, her purse slung over her shoulder, a chipper, "Ready to go!" bursting from her lips.

He always felt the most like himself—whoever that was—around Sydney.

Until Marley.

He shook his head to clear that thought and focused on Syd. "How's school?"

She took a sip of water. "I thought classes would be harder once I got to high school."

He raised his eyebrows. "I'm sure it will get harder each

year."

She shrugged. "Maybe. Dad says I must have somehow inherited your brain."

Austin thought about how to respond to that. His brain had made him rich, but lately it hadn't quite made him happy. He was distrustful and obsessive and antisocial, whereas Sydney was friendly and personable. "Well, you inherited your father's charm, and I think that's more beneficial."

Sydney cocked her head and grinned. "You think I'm charming?"

"Don't be cute."

She giggled and held out the chip bag. He shook his head to decline and she stuck her hand back in for more chips. "Dad said you should date."

The girl had no filter. "Did he now? I'm sure he said that without the intention of me hearing it."

Sydney leaned closer. "Probably. He was talking to Grandma. But I think you should hear it."

Austin snorted. "Of course you do."

"Grandma also said you need to loosen your tie a little and take the stick out of your ass."

Well, ouch. That hurt. Grant's mother was just like him; they didn't mince words. "Don't say ass."

"You just said it."

He glared at her.

"He also said that maybe you like men."

For the love of God. "Did they say all this in front of you?"

Sydney rolled her eyes. "No, I was supposed to be doing homework this morning, but I had my ear against the door of my bedroom so I could hear them talking."

"Of course you did."

"So do you like men?"

He exhaled slowly. "I like men but I'm not attracted to them sexually."

Sydney thought on that a minute. "Oh."

Should he have gotten permission from Grant to talk to her about this? Oh, whatever. Grant's fault for not talking quieter, the jackass.

Sydney was still talking. "What about that woman at the movie theater?"

Oh, dammit. "What about her?"

"She was pretty. I liked her hair."

Austin liked more than her hair. "Yes, she is pretty."

Sydney was an old soul. Her eyes looked wise in her fourteen-year-old face. "Is she funny?"

Austin laughed—a deep laugh from his belly—because yes, his Evelyn was quite funny. "She is, Syd."

His niece's face lit up. "That's great! That's what you need, then. A woman who makes you laugh and smile."

That sobered him up a little. "Why do you say that?"

She shrugged. "I don't think you do it enough."

He poked her in the side. "I laugh with you."

She rolled her eyes. "You know what I mean."

"You don't think I laugh enough?"

Sydney picked at a loose thread in her jeans. "I just think sometimes you seem lonely."

In the past, he'd always said that he preferred to be by himself. He'd grown up lonely, with only his father for company. So he maintained the status quo, really only letting Grant and Sydney close.

But everyone else? No. They were kept at arm's length—

an arm clothed in a starched shirt with platinum cufflinks.

Lately, he'd been questioning this lifestyle of solitude. And just when he thought he could let Marley in, he had to keep his distance from her for her own good. Wasn't that depressing?

He swallowed and stared ahead, not really seeing anything. "Sometimes I guess I am lonely."

That confession seemed to perk up Syd. "So you'll ask her on a date?"

He smiled sadly. "Won't work out with her, I'm afraid."

Syd's face fell. "Oh."

"How about this?" He wanted to make her happy, even if it was an insane promise. "I'll ask a woman out this month, okay? I'll go on a date this month." At the rate he was going, he might have to pay a woman, but dammit, he'd do it.

Sydney beamed. "Great!"

He wondered how much he'd regret this promise. And he also wished he could date the woman he really wanted.

They talked for another hour or so and then it was time to take Sydney home.

Usually on his days with Syd, he dropped her off without visiting Grant. But today, Grant must have heard his car, because he opened the front door and leaned against the frame, arms crossed over his chest, staring at Austin through the windshield. He wore an old college T-shirt and a pair of sweatpants. Ethan's black tank of a Range Rover was parked at the curb.

"I think my dad wants to talk to you," Sydney said from the passenger seat.

"Yeah? What gave you that impression?" he muttered as he turned the car off and opened his door.

Sydney hopped out and gave her dad a high five, then low five as she walked past him, their ritual the same since she learned what a high five was.

She waved over her shoulder to Austin, "Thanks, Uncle A! Got homework to do." Then she disappeared into the house.

Austin stuck his hands in the pockets of his jeans and slowly walked up the stairs of Grant's porch. He waited for Grant to talk, which wasn't long. It never was.

"Want some coffee?" Grant asked, straightening from the frame and dropping his hands at his sides.

Austin shook his head.

Grant rolled his eyes. "Just come inside. I want to talk to you."

"You could have just said that," Austin said, walking past Grant into the house.

He didn't have to turn around to know Grant was making a face at the back of his head.

He wandered into the kitchen and lifted the lid on the cookie jar. Sydney was in to baking and always had some sort of fresh dessert. It was good for her, too, because many baked goods contained peanuts and weren't safe for her to eat. Grant bitched about his waistline, but still ate every treat Sydney dreamed up. Austin reached inside and pulled out a brownie square with caramel drizzle.

"Help yourself," Grant said, leaning a hand on the kitchen counter.

"Always do," Austin said around a mouthful of chocolate. "Wow, these are good."

Grant grabbed one out of the jar and took a bite. "I know, kid's going to turn me into a blimp."

Austin ignored the comment. Grant was his age, thirty-two. His hair was just as thick as it had been in college, the same golden blonde, and the guy still worked out every day. He wasn't in danger of a thickening waistband any more than he was in danger of settling down. Grant enjoyed his variety in women as much as his desserts. "Where's Ethan?"

Grant looked confused. "How'd you know Ethan was here?"

Austin swallowed his last bite of brownie and talked slowly. "His tank is parked outside your house."

Grant's face lit up. "Oh yeah. Of course. Sorry. I'm a little…" He waved a hand and stuck out his tongue. "…today."

Austin didn't mention that he was a little that way every day.

"Anyway, we were watching the game, and he had a phone call."

Ethan's footsteps announced his arrival. He entered the kitchen in a pair of jeans and a hooded sweatshirt pulled snug around his neck. Austin could still see the burn scars, creeping up to lick at the underside of his jaw.

He nodded at Austin, his pale blue eyes cool as always. At least, since Austin had known him. Apparently he hadn't been like that, before the accident that had permanently turned Ethan into the recluse he was now. Austin rarely saw Ethan, had truthfully only met him once or twice, and wondered how Grant got him to leave his home. He must have bribed him with brownies.

Ethan walked right over to the cookie jar and pulled out a brownie.

Yep, Grant bribed him with brownies.

Ethan took a bite and then leaned back on the counter.

"How was your date with Syd?"

"Good."

"What'd you do?"

The small talk was making them both uncomfortable. "Had a picnic at the park."

"Fascinating conversation," Grant interrupted. "But what I really want to hear is…" He lowered his voice. "'Yes, Ethan, I'd love a whole lot of money. I'll definitely sell you my half of *Gamers*.'" Grant lowered his voice even more. "'Great, Austin. I can't wait to work with Grant because he's so smart and handsome. Thanks for blessing me with the opportunity.'" Then Grant spoke in his regular tone, "Then you handshake, and everyone is happy."

Austin glared at Grant, who smiled back at him with a lot of teeth.

"I said I'd think about it," Austin said. He turned to Ethan. "Why do you want to get involved in this?"

Ethan raised an eyebrow. "Is this an interrogation?"

Grant's gaze ping-ponged between the two of them, like he could be called in any minute to pull them apart.

"This business is important to Grant and me," Austin said carefully. "I want to make sure it's in the right hands."

Ethan didn't move for a minute, his cool eyes boring into Austin. They were like two bucks about to clash antlers. Ethan's jaw moved as he chewed, and then he swallowed his brownie. "So what you're saying is that you don't think mine are the right hands."

Austin had to give it to the guy, he didn't back down. "Well, I—"

"Okay," Grant stepped in. "The temperature in this room is about twenty degrees lower than I ever allow my balls to get, so can we cut the crap? Ethan wants the business and he'll do a great job with it, Austin. I trust him."

Ethan didn't take his eyes off of Austin. "Someone has to keep Grant in line."

"Hey!" Grant protested.

Austin needed to let this go. He was in Grant's house with Sydney nearby and his puffing chest routine with Ethan didn't belong here. So he backed down. Reluctantly. "I'll let you know by the end of the month." He had a lot of things to do this month now. Like find a date. His stomach rolled just thinking about it. "The game still on?"

Ethan checked his watch. "Halftime should be about over."

Austin nodded and walked to the refrigerator. He grabbed three beers, handing one to Grant and another to Ethan, keeping the third to himself. "I think I'd rather watch football than discuss business."

Grant's eyebrows rose into his hairline. "Austin doesn't want to talk business? Are pigs flying?"

Ethan snorted and Austin gave them the finger over his shoulder as he walked to the living room.

Chapter Eight

Marley sucked on her straw, catching the last of her Long Island Iced Tea until the straw gasped and gurgled from lack of liquid.

She set it on the table and glared at it. It was her second, and she still wasn't drunk enough to deal with this.

Chad was on the dance floor, grinding with some woman who wore a short skirt and a top that looked suspiciously like lingerie.

Marley sighed and looked around the bar.

Dance clubs were so not her thing. The bass of the music slammed into her skull like a hammer, the strobe lights hurt her eyes, and all she could smell was alcohol, sweat, and cologne. *The Cherry* on a Thursday was barely tolerable. *The Cherry* on a Saturday was mind-numbing. Why had she agreed to come? She'd rather be home watching *Die Hard* on Blu-ray with Sadie.

The smack of a palm on the table jolted her from her

musings. Chad plopped down in the booth next to her. He handed her another drink, which was the only thing that made *The Cherry* worthwhile tonight. They truly made the best Long Island Ice Teas. The drink knocked her on her ass, but that was probably what she needed because she sure as hell wasn't getting her hands on an ass any time soon.

Which only made her think of Austin.

Which brought her back to the reason she was drinking in the first place. *Full circle, Mars*, she thought.

"Okay," Chad said. "You have two drunk stages depending on your mood before imbibing. We either get happy, giggly Marley who tells lame newspaper jokes, like what's black and white and red all over—"

"That joke is timeless—"

"Or we get sad, moaning Marley who listens to Smashing Pumpkins and reminisces about her goth, emo high school years."

"Hey, my eyeliner game was on point in high school," she protested.

Chad rolled his eyes. "And I'm thinking we're going to get Billy Corgan-like Marley tonight because you're still moping about losing out on that hot computer stud who tapped your home keys."

"I thought we talked about these puns."

"I thought we talked about how I will never stop." Chad took a sip of his water. "So, are you going to admit how you've been in a funk all week because of a certain man?"

She was just drunk enough to be stubborn as hell. "I'm stressed about work. I didn't even miss his dirty emails."

That was a lie. She sipped on her straw. "I also didn't avoid the supply closet in any way."

That was another lie.

Chad raised his eyebrows.

She refused to admit she ached for Austin's touch. She needed to stop pining after this guy. "Your job, Marley," she chanted to herself. "Remember your job."

"What the hell? Are you talking to yourself?" Chad laid the back of his hand on her forehead, like he was testing her for fever.

She swatted his hand away. "I'm fine." Another lie? "And to show you how fine I am, I'm going to go find a man on that dance floor, and I'm going to debase myself with him to prove it."

Chad swept his arm in front of him, gesturing toward the dance floor. "Be my guest, Mars. I better see tongue and boob-grabbage."

She huffed and stood up, a little unsteady on her feet. She decided stiletto heels were a bad idea when she planned to wallow in a corner with Long Island Iced Teas lined up in front of her.

She shook her hair over her shoulder and walked with as much balance as she could muster onto the dance floor.

It was a club, full of drunk people, so it wasn't like it was hard to find a man willing to grab her by the hips and grind his crotch into her ass.

She guessed he was cute, but it was kind of hard to tell. She had beer goggles. Or Long Island Iced Tea goggles, which she assumed were even more skewed. But he had hair and facial features and all his limbs, so what the hell. She went with it.

She closed her eyes and tried to let the beat of the music take her away. The man behind her heated her back, and his thighs pressed into hers, a hand at her waist, those fingertips digging through the thin fabric of her dress.

"You're hot," he said in her ear. And she couldn't stop her flinch. Because that voice was wrong. Those words were wrong.

Her body screamed at her to pull away, to go sit back down at her table and drink more alcohol until every touch felt like Austin's. But she knew that wasn't going to happen. He'd ruined her, hadn't he? With that low, soft voice, the way he told her she was beautiful, the way he looked at her like she was precious. The way he played her body like he'd been born to bring her pleasure. As much as she loved her job, how could she deny herself what Austin did for her? She'd been denying herself for years, putting her career before her own pleasure. And really, what was the point?

And if…they made sure to keep their interactions far away from *Gamers*, well then, maybe she could have her cake and eat it too.

She popped her eyes open and stopped dancing. She stood frozen as the man behind her slowly came to a halt. "You okay, baby? Want a drink?"

She stared at Chad as he stood up and began to walk toward her, his brows furrowed in concern.

The hand left her hip, and its owner must have spotted Chad, because he said, "You got a nice little body, sweetheart, but I'm not getting involved with you and your boyfriend."

His heat left her back and she exhaled, realizing how tense she'd been, how much his touch had actually repulsed her. And it wasn't his fault. It was Austin's. Damn that man.

Chad reached her side and grabbed her hand. "You okay, Mars?"

She looked up into her brother's eyes. "I want to go home."

Chad kept glancing at her while he drove back to her apartment, but she was busy doing important things, like squinting at her phone.

She didn't have Austin's number. She thought about looking him up on White Pages but didn't feel like searching through a dozen Austin Rivers duds.

So she pulled up her email and began typing.

"What are you doing over there?" Chad asked.

"Typing." Oops, she erased a letter when she tried to type "m". Stupid small keyboards.

"What are you typing, Mars?" His voice was cautious.

"An email."

"I—"

"Just shut it, Chad. You got me drunk and now this is the end result, me emailing a guy who's now given me, like, three orgasms, but yet I don't have his number."

Chad shut up.

And Marley kept typing.

Austin sat at his desk and rubbed his forehead. The headache was forming, the one that told him he needed to quit working and go to bed.

It was Saturday and he'd been working all day. Well, not really working, more like staring at his computer screen and trying to decide if he wanted to sell *Gamers* or not. Why was this so hard? Grant was happy with Ethan as a business partner, so why couldn't Austin pull the damn trigger?

He sighed and went to shut down his computer for the night, when he saw he had an email. He figured it was junk, until he noticed it was to his Aricofthelobby account. He had set it up that all those emails came to his main inbox.

And the only person who had that address?

Marley.

There was no subject. He took a deep breath and clicked to open the email.

i tried so hard but i can't stop. thinking of you. we never got the chance to see if i could come just from your voice.

i want that chance.

He wasn't breathing. If he were asthmatic, he'd be grabbing his inhaler.

She wanted that chance. And fuck, he couldn't deny he wanted it too. He wasn't done with Marley. She had more fantasies and he wanted to give them to her. He'd be her Sexual Fantasy Ambassador.

Well, that title wasn't so sexy. He wouldn't bring that up around her.

But it had to be him. He was born to touch her body, to see her flushed and sated. The thought of another man with his hand around her throat....

Austin growled. A real, honest to God growl.

He lunged across his desk for his phone, knocking it to the ground so he had to crawl under his desk to retrieve it. He bumped his head on his way back into his chair and swore.

His heart was racing and his hands were sweaty. He almost dropped the phone again.

In Marley's email, she'd given him her phone number. He could have signed into *Gamers'* electronic employee file and found her number. But that was weird, so he was glad he didn't have to do that.

The phone rang six times and went to her voicemail. Austin swore again, rubbed his head, and tried again.

This time she answered, sounding breathless.

"Hello?"

Austin bit down on his lip, hard, until he heard a crunch.

"Hello?" She giggled. "Who is this?"

He released his lip. "Do you still want that chance?"

A small gasp, just a quick intake of air. "Austin."

He closed his eyes, soaking in the way she said his name, the way she drew out the first syllable, pausing on the "s" and rolling it around on her tongue before it slipped off.

No one said his name like that. And he didn't want anyone else to.

Only Marley.

He heard a couple of thumps in the background, a rustling of keys. "Where are you?"

"I'm home now."

A voice in the background, masculine. Austin tensed. "You're not alone?"

"It's just my brother, he's leaving now." There was a smile in her voice, and then Austin heard a slam of the door.

"You didn't answer my question," he said softly.

Another noise, this one sounded like a moan. "Yes."

"Yes what?"

A pause. Austin could hear every second tick on the swinging pendulum of the grandfather clock in his office.

"Yes, I'd like that chance."

"Now?"

"Now."

Austin was already on the way to his bedroom. "Then let's do it, sweetheart."

She made that sound again in the back of her throat.

"Where are you?" he asked. He sank into the soft chair in the corner of his bedroom and spread his legs, palming his erection through his dress pants. He wanted to draw this out, make them both crazy.

"I'm…in my living room. On my couch."

"Are you near a window?" He wanted that feeling, that anyone could be watching while she touched herself to the sound of his voice. But no one else could touch. No way. Not ever, if he had it his way.

"Yes," she gasped. "I-I have a big bay window."

"Are the curtains open?"

A pause, then a breathy, "Yes."

She liked that, his Marley. "Good, now what are you wearing?" He flicked open the top button of his pants.

"A dress."

"What does it look like?"

"It's…um…a short dress, blue, and I'm wearing heels."

"What's under the dress, sweetheart?"

"A…lace thong. Pale blue."

He closed his eyes. Pale blue, like the tie he'd used to cover her eyes. "Hike up your skirt and spread your legs."

"O-Okay."

He imagined her on her couch, legs spread, the muscles

in her calves and thighs flexing, heels on the floor. Skirt at her waist, head thrown back. Her fingers slipping beneath the edge of that lacy fabric. "Touch yourself. Tell me what you feel."

He could hear the swallow in her voice. "Austin…"

"Tell me, Evelyn."

Her breath caught, then she exhaled into her phone. "I feel…wet. God, Austin."

He lowered the zipper of his pants. "Tell me why you're wet."

"Because…of your voice. And the memory of you touching me."

"You want that again?" He peeled away the flaps of his pants and pulled his hard, aching cock out of his boxers.

"Yes."

"What do you want? My fingers or my mouth?"

She made a strangled sound.

"Don't come yet. Stop touching yourself if you're close."

"Please," she whimpered.

"If I was there right now, I'd smack that swollen clit of yours, to remind you that you don't come without me saying so."

"Yes."

"Smack it for me. Hold yourself open. Let me hear it."

He listened for it, that wet slap. And when the sound came, he wrapped his fist around his cock and squeezed. "Fuck, Marley."

"Austin. I want your mouth," she whispered.

He still didn't trust himself, so he kept a grip on his cock to the point of pain. "I'm there, on my knees between your thighs. You're not allowed to touch me. I kiss the inside of each thigh, lick the skin there. You taste like heaven, Marley, did you know that?"

"N-No."

"Well, you do. And now I'm pushing your knees farther apart. I need a lot of room to work, Marley. I'm gripping your hips, and with my thumbs, I'm opening you up. I want to see you, all swollen and wet for me. You are, aren't you?"

"God, yes."

"And now, I'm pulling you toward me. Your skirt is at your waist, your thong is off and I'm staring at my present. I'm staring at my feast."

She gasped and said some words that didn't sound like English.

Austin swiped his thumb over his slit, gathering a drop of pre-cum, and then began to stroke his cock. "I'm shoving my head between your thighs. And I'm taking one, long lick."

She groaned.

"And now, Marley, now, I'm feasting. I can taste you on my tongue. I'm holding onto your hips while you grind your-self on my mouth. You're all over my face, and I'm working you with my tongue and lips."

"Oh my God."

Austin moved his hand faster. He'd brought her to or-gasm three times now. He knew what she sounded like when she was close, the way her voice rose. "Touch yourself. Put two fingers inside your pussy. Imagine it's my tongue. And rub that clit with your thumb. Do it, Marley."

"Oh fuck," she said, her breath coming in pants now.

"Tell me."

"I'm so wet, and I'm so close."

He could feel it too, his balls tightening up, wanting,

needing to release. "Come for me, I'll lap it all up, sweetheart. Come in my mouth."

There was no sound, just silence, and then her voice broke through, a loud curse and then his name, "Auuuustin. Oh *God*!"

That was all he needed, his name from her lips in the throes of an orgasm. He came with a whispered curse, his hand working his cock as he shot all over his pants and stomach.

He was slumped in his chair, covered in his release, panting into the phone while Marley made small gasps on the other end.

He should hang up, before he did something crazy, like propose. He imagined her lying on her couch, beautiful breasts rising and falling, bare ass exposed, curls a mess. If he was there, he'd lay behind her, one hand on a breast, the other possessively cupping her wet, sensitive skin between her legs. He'd dip a finger in her folds while she squirmed, and he'd leave it there, keeping that connection.

Yeah, he needed to get off the phone. He opened his mouth, unsure what to say now that the urgent need to come had evaporated. He'd never had phone sex before. Was there etiquette?

Marley shifted on the other end and when she spoke, her voice was soft and a little slurred. "Thanks for that chance."

And then she hung up. The silence on the other line was deafening in Austin's ear.

The next day, Austin found himself cornered in Grant's kitchen by Sydney. He'd borrowed Grant's wet vac a couple of weeks ago and finally got around to returning it. Or maybe he just wanted out of his house, because being alone with thoughts of Marley was driving him insane.

But he hadn't counted on the tenacity of a teenage girl.

"So, do you have a date lined up this month yet?" She tore a piece off of her muffin, which smelled delicious, and stuffed it into her mouth. She'd informed him she'd made cranberry-orange muffins, but he didn't get one until he coughed up details about his love life.

The girl was pure evil.

"I do not." He wasn't going to kowtow to her.

She stuck out her lower lip, and his resolve began to crack. God, he was weak. Over a pout and a muffin.

He clenched his jaw. "I have a solid lead, though."

Sydney rolled her eyes. "I can't believe you just spoke of a possible date as a 'solid lead.'"

"It's an accurate description of the situation," he explained, as his gaze darted to the pan of muffins.

"Nuh-uh-uh," Sydney said. "You didn't earn your muffin."

Austin narrowed his eyes. "I don't like you."

Grant walked in to the kitchen, in his normal Sunday attire of cutoff sweatpants and an old college T-shirt with a huge hole in the left armpit. He picked a muffin off the tray and shoved half of it into his mouth, chewing as crumbs fell to the floor.

Austin salivated.

Sydney raised an eyebrow.

Grant frowned and brushed some crumbs off of his chest.

After the phone call last night, Austin had spent a lot of time pacing. He wanted to call Marley back and ask her out properly. He wanted to delve into more of her fantasies, and he wanted to get to know her. Which was a novel concept for him, but there it was, plain as day. So it wasn't a hard decision. Plus, he wanted that damn muffin. Austin threw up his hands. "Okay, fine. You win, devil child. I'll ask her out on a date, okay?"

"When?" she demanded.

"Today." He'd text Marley. Or email. Whatever he got up the nerve to do. But he'd do it.

Sydney pointed to the tray of treats. "Do you actually want to go out with her or are you just doing this for the baked goods?"

A whole night with Marley. Her attention on him, her soft curves under his hands. Austin didn't even hesitate. "I want her."

Sydney blinked at his answer. "Okay, you may proceed to the nearest muffin."

Austin grabbed one before Sydney changed her mind. Of course, he ate it with manners, unlike Grant. He wasn't an animal.

Chapter Nine

The text had come on Sunday, right as Marley was curling up on the couch with Sadie, a bowl of reheated soup in her hand.

I'd like to take you out. Please be ready Saturday at 8 PM.

He'd even added the PM, as if she really thought he'd start a date at 8 AM. It was adorable.

She'd spent the whole morning wondering what the hell he was thinking about her email and their smutty phone call, so this text was a relief.

Her response was, *I'll be ready.*

The week had passed in a daze—one in which Marley went to bed hearing Austin's voice, feeling his hands on her skin, and woke up aching and unsatisfied.

She recognized this was crazy and reckless. And maybe that's what made it so appealing. She vowed she'd get her head on straight next week, after this night with Austin.

After glancing at the clock in her bedroom, she slipped a diamond stud into her pierced ear. He'd be there in fifteen minutes. At least, that's what his email said. He'd told her to wear a dress.

She should have bristled at being told what to wear, but instead she was grateful because at least it narrowed down her clothing choices considerably. Less stress that way.

Which was greatly appreciated. It'd been a trying week at work, with Marley rushing to put out fire after fire. One of her copy editors had discovered a major factual error in an article which had been deemed finished, and another one of her staff found a screen grab of a video game was not the one mentioned in the article. On top of that, one freelancer had submitted his story with incorrect links, then seemed to vanish, so Marley spent a good two hours she didn't have tracking down the correct URLs.

By the end of the week, she was barely hanging on. Her voice hurt from firing off directives and the last thing she wanted to do was think or make any more decisions. James had been pleased with her handling of each situation and even bought her lunch on Friday. But a date with Austin seemed like the best medicine for her week from hell.

He'd only emailed her that once, even though she wished for his dirty words in her inbox. None came. But hopefully, she'd get the dirty words in person tonight. Her imagination was starting to run dry.

It was amazing how he'd filtered into her life like vapor, so he was everywhere all at once, in all things she did.

She smoothed down her skirt and checked out her outfit in her floor length mirror. She'd chosen a simple, slimming red dress that hugged all her curves. A silver chain hung from her neck, a small sword pendant dangling from the end. She'd bought it this week because it reminded her of *Aric's Revenge*, which would also bring up thoughts of Austin. She wondered if he'd notice.

She'd chosen the highest heels she had—black patent leather stilettos. She'd paired them with a pair of black thigh-highs. What was underneath the dress was for Austin. She grinned and fiddled with her hair at her shoulders. After one more sweep of powder on her face, neck, and chest, she walked downstairs to wait for Austin's knock.

She had no idea if he was normally punctual. She looked forward to finding that out, plus a lot more about him. She knew his body and she knew he could play hers like an instrument. But other than that, he was a mystery.

She was idly straightening some throw pillows on her couch—and frowning at a stain she was sure had been made by Chad—when her doorbell rang.

Marley took a deep breath and walked over to the door, her heels clicking loudly on her hardwood floors.

When she opened it, Austin stood holding a bouquet of flowers. He wore a black suit but no tie, his white shirt open at the collar. His dark hair was combed back, and Marley spotted small streaks of gray at his temples. Damn, that was hot.

She reached out her hand and took the bouquet, which was elaborate. It was brimming with flowers she'd never seen before and—was that an artichoke?—the stem was wrapped in pale blue silk. She bit her lip. Just the sight of that color now was enough to make her dizzy.

"They're gorgeous. Thank you, Austin."

He didn't say anything. His gaze roaming her hair, face, cleavage, and then down her legs felt like fingers.

When his gaze met hers, he smiled. "You look beautiful."

She blushed. Actually blushed. When was the last time she did that? When was the last time anyone had called her beautiful? "Thank you. Let me go put these in water and then we'll…go do whatever you have planned. You can come in."

He took a step inside and shut the door behind him. She turned on her heel, nose in the bouquet as she made her way to the kitchen. She pulled a vase down off a shelf when he spoke again. "Dinner."

She turned around with the vase clutched in one hand, the bouquet in the other. "Excuse me?"

He licked his lips then seemed to shake himself. He pushed back the edges of his suit jacket and shoved his hands in his pockets. "I'm taking you to dinner. I thought… I'm not sure I've made such a good impression so far. And you deserve to be treated well." He cleared his throat. "Very well."

She blinked at him as his words sank in. She turned to face the counter and began to fill the vase with water from her sink. She wished she could stick her face under the cool stream because she was burning up already. After the vase was full, she set it down and slipped the bouquet inside. "You don't have to do that. I'm fine with Sour Patch Kids and a movie."

When she turned back around, he looked confused, uncertain. She suppressed a smile. He was a computer guy, a video game nerd. She was sure he liked everything organized, compartmentalized. He would have planned this date because, in his mind, that's what a man did—buy a woman dinner. Wine and dine her.

And she'd just thrown him for a loop.

She walked toward him and laid a hand on his forearm. She placed a kiss on his chin, the only place she could reach. "This is nice, Austin. I'd love dinner."

That seemed to satisfy him. His face lightened, and he nodded. Then he cocked his elbow for her to take his arm. "Then we should get going. I have reservations."

Of course he did. She smiled to herself as she grabbed her clutch off the counter and walked with him toward the door. His planning was cute. Although, she was sure he'd take his palm to her ass if she called him cute.

A jolt of heat shot through her. She made a mental note to call him cute later.

He opened her car door for her, then walked around the hood and settled into the driver's seat. She enjoyed the feel of the leather seats on her legs, the gentle vibrations of the car under her.

She didn't ask where they were going. They could have kept driving all night, to be honest. They had made it out of her small suburb now and were heading into the city. She watched the lights go past in the passenger window. He asked about her week and she told him about all of the uncharacteristic issues that had cropped up and how she solved them. "I just hope James made a note of every single one of these and uses them when he's deciding who gets the promotion."

Austin patted her thigh. "I'm sure he will."

She hoped so. Jack Sorrel, normally a lazy piece of crap, had all of a sudden come alive, walking around with page proofs in his hands, looking important and barking orders at no one in particular. If he got the job over her, she'd spit.

She glanced at Austin as the fading light poured through the windshield. She wondered if Jack would make a scene if he found out about Austin. It bothered her, like a splinter under her skin, but she shoved it aside. It was just one date, right?

You're falling for him, said a voice in her head. But she shoved it aside.

"What would be a dream date for you?" Austin asked, taking her out of her thoughts.

"A dream date?"

He gripped the steering wheel and a muscle in his jaw tensed when he nodded.

She thought about it for a minute. "Well, there's a Comic-Con coming up in Philadelphia. Did you hear about that?"

He glanced at her, then nodded again.

She smiled. "That would be a perfect date. We'd cosplay. You'd be Aric and I'd be Evelyn. How hot would you be in Aric's leather pants, swinging a big sword around?" She giggled, on a roll now. "And I'd braid my hair and wear Evelyn's corset, with cleavage busting out and that cool skirt with a slit up to my thigh, a knife tucked into my garter. Don't you think that would be fun?"

She looked over at him as they stopped at a red light. He was facing straight ahead, his lips pressed into a thin line. "Austin?"

He swallowed. "Uh, I'm not really into that kind of thing."

She frowned. "Comic-Cons?"

"No. Well, yeah, I'm not really into that either. But I don't…cosplay. I don't like attention or crowds." He blew out a breath and Marley didn't have the heart to be irritated. The guy looked flat-out terrified. He turned his head to face her. "I'm very sorry about that."

She was disappointed. Of course she was. Chad had gone with her a couple of times, but she always dreamed of going with her boyfriend or husband. They'd dress up together and then sneak off somewhere to have sex all dressed up.

But that wouldn't happen with Austin. And that was okay. She didn't want to go on a date that would be torture for him. That wouldn't be fun for anyone. "You don't have to be sorry. It was just a stupid little idea." She waved her hand.

He reached out and grabbed her fingers as the light turned green. He didn't move the car. "It's not stupid, Marley. It's not stupid at all. I'm sorry but that's just…not me."

She smiled. "I know. It's okay, Austin. Really."

A car honked behind them and irritation flashed over Austin's face before he let go of her hand and took his foot off the brake. "I'll make it up to you."

"There's nothing to make up—"

"Marley," he said, and this time when he looked at her, his beautiful eyes held a little bit of vulnerability. "Tonight, I want you to understand how well you deserve to be treated. And that I can be the man to do it."

The things he said. Except this wasn't dirty talk that sent heat right between her legs. This caused a bloom of warmth in her chest. Near her heart.

She closed her eyes. This was their first real date. She had to get it together and not dream about forever already.

When she opened her eyes, he glanced at her. She smiled. "Okay, Austin."

He smiled back, and held her hand on the rest of the

way to the restaurant.

He pulled into the parking lot of Vito's. Marley raised her brows. She'd never eaten there before, and heard it was difficult to get reservations. Although, really, was she surprised in any way that Austin had pulled it off?

No.

He had a way about him that made people eager to do his bidding. It didn't seem like it was just her. She glanced back at his car as they walked toward the front doors of the restaurant. He drove a Jaguar—a new one, from the looks of it. She tried to think of a way to ask her next question without seeming like a gold digging busy body. She only wanted to know him better—what interested him and what made him tick. "So I don't see you at *Gamers* much."

He cleared his throat. "I only work there part-time."

"So it's not your only job?"

Austin stared straight ahead. "I dabble in other things."

She bit her lip so she didn't giggle at his use of the word *dabble*. "Like real estate?"

He opened the door and ushered her inside with his hand on the small of her back. "Something like that."

He was being kind of cagey, so a niggle of doubt tickled at the back of her brain. She trusted him with her body, since he'd shown her time and again he knew how to pleasure her the way she craved. But where would this relationship go? It wasn't only about sex anymore if he was taking her out on a date, was it? And what if she got attached? Could she trust him with her heart? She turned to face him. "Is it illegal?"

He barked out a laugh and pressed his lips to her forehead. "I promise I'm a law-abiding citizen."

She let it go, then.

Inside Vito's, it was all creams and golds, low candlelight flickering on the tables. She walked among the tables, following the hostess. Austin's hand lay on the small of her back, guiding her, yet his fingers were curled into her in a way that was possessive. Claiming. She loved it.

The hostess led them to a booth in the back corner. The light was even lower there and, while the restaurant was full, the nearest tables weren't easily visible once they slid into the cool leather. Austin's body crowded her into the corner, and she thanked the waiter for handing her the menu.

She opened the thick menu, the outside covered in some sort of fabric, and ran her finger down the cream paper, where all the dishes were listed in scripted font.

No prices.

"Do you like wine?" Austin asked.

She wanted to snort out a laugh, but that wasn't very ladylike and maybe a little inappropriate for a restaurant as nice as this. So she said, "Yes, of course."

"Red?"

"That's fine."

He ordered a fancy-sounding wine, and the waiter scurried off to supply it.

Austin finally opened up his menu. He glanced at it for about thirty seconds before shutting it and putting it aside.

She hadn't even made it through the appetizers. "Do you know what you want already?"

He looked at her, and the flame from the candle sparked on the gold flecks in his eyes. "Yes."

She frowned at her menu. "That was quick. I have no idea what I want. What are you getting?"

He seemed amused by her, his lips tipped up on one side. He pointed to a line on the menu, and she squinted at the words. "*Mussels Fra Diavolo.*" There were no descriptions of the dishes. "What's that?"

He leaned an elbow on the table and braced his head on his fingers. "Mussels in a spicy red sauce."

"Don't put your elbow on the table."

A bigger smile now. "Why?"

"I don't know! My mom always said you didn't put your elbows on the table. Didn't your mother ever tell you that?"

He stared at her, then slowly took his elbow off of the table. "No, she didn't."

Marley sighed. "Well, my mom always harped on the etiquette stuff. I'm not good at it, despite all her nagging. So your mom wasn't like that?"

She didn't mean anything by the question, just conversation. Weren't parents a safe conversation starter? Apparently not, because Austin's face hardened slightly. "I wouldn't know. Never met her. She left my father shortly after I was born."

She'd stepped in it, hadn't she? *Good job, Mars.* "I'm sorry to have brought that up, Austin."

He placed a hand at the nape of her neck and rubbed her skin with his thumb. "It's okay. You didn't know."

The waiter arrived with their wine, pouring a small amount in Austin's glass for him to taste. He did, and nodded, so the waiter topped him off, then filled Marley's glass. He left with a small bow.

Marley looked over at Austin, who wore a small furrow

between his brows. He hadn't revealed much about his personal life until this moment, and with this admission about his mother, that niggle in the back of her brain began to fade. "I bet you want me to change the subject, don't you?" she said.

That brought his smile back. "That'd be nice."

She looked back at the menu. "Okay, so…can I just get chicken?"

Austin threw back his head and laughed, the sound booming into the restaurant. "I take you to Vito's, which has a month wait list for reservations and serves thousand dollar wine and you want chicken?" He didn't sound annoyed, he sounded thoroughly entertained.

She placed a hand on his thigh. "This restaurant is gorgeous, and the smells coming from the kitchen are making my mouth water. But I just don't know…what food to order. I see *pollo* and I get excited and then I can't figure out what all these words are after it."

He was laughing again.

"Quit laughing at me! I don't know Italian! I'm from Pennsylvania Dutch Country!"

He laughed harder, slapping his hand on the table so the silverware rattled.

She glared at him until he was quiet, wiping his tear-stained cheeks. "Are you done?" she huffed.

He leaned in closer, his thigh pressed against hers. "I failed big time on this date, didn't I?"

That was the last thing she wanted him to think. Especially because she'd never seen him this animated and laughing, even if it was at her expense. She couldn't stop grinning as she watched this playful side of Austin he so rarely showed. "No! I swear. I love it."

"You'd love it more of we were getting comic books signed while dressed as... Han Solo and Princess Leia."

"That's kind of unoriginal," she muttered.

"I guess I'll have to take other measures to improve this date." He leaned in, his breath hot on her neck. She squirmed as he whispered, "Hands on the table."

She jerked her head up and looked at him, then peeked around the restaurant. No one was watching them, but still...

"Austin," she hissed.

"Keep your hands on the table," he said as he flicked her earlobe with his nose. "You had a long week, in which you showed everyone how good you are at your job. Now, my job is to take control and give you what you need. And I'm quite good at my job."

Her hands shook in her lap. "Austin—"

"You saying my name like that isn't helping your case."

She bit her lip and laid her palms flat on the table. Then she clasped them together in front of her, interlocking her fingers, because that was the only way to keep them in place as his palm slid up the inside of her thigh.

He reached the lace at the top of her thigh-highs and stopped. She smiled to herself as his questing fingers found the clasp connected to her garter belt. He hissed under his breath. "I see that smile. You wore these for me?"

"Of course I did." Her voice shook as he slid a finger under the strap and snapped it against her skin. "Austin..."

"Shhhh, no one can see. We're in a corner by ourselves and the cloth on the table hides what I'm doing to you underneath it."

She breathed, yoga-style, in through her nose, out through

her mouth as his hands continued up her inner thigh. "And what are you doing?"

He leaned over and kissed her jaw, just as his hand cupped her over her panties. "I'm going to do my job and enjoy what's mine."

She bit back the moan, clamping her molars down on the inside of her cheeks. He pressed his hand against her harder. "And you like that idea, don't you? Because I can feel how wet you are. I can feel you soaking through this lace."

She squirmed, and he chuckled.

"So for now, you'll get my fingers. After dinner, if you're good, you'll get my cock."

She was breathing hard now, like she'd just run a marathon. Austin was the best workout ever. A finger ran along the crease of her thigh and slipped under the edge of her panties. "Are you going to be good?"

She rotated her hips, and thrust slightly into his hand. She licked her lips and turned to look at him. "I'll be very good."

His gaze was on her lips. "That's what I like to hear."

The waiter arrived at their table with a smile. Austin took it easy on her, his fingers only tracing the edge of her panties as she stumbled over ordering something with *pollo* in it. She had no idea if Austin actually ordered those mussels, because she wasn't paying attention. She took that opportunity to gulp as much wine as she could.

The waiter looked at her funny and she smiled brightly at him. Probably too brightly, edging on maniacal. Oh well, he didn't understand what it was like to sit in a restaurant with a man's hand down his pants.

Or maybe he did.

She shook her head as the waiter walked away.

Austin continued gently tracing that boundary, where lace met skin. She rolled her hips slightly, urging, and Austin tutted under his breath. "You said you'd be good."

She clenched her hands on the table, her knuckles white. "I'm trying, but you're driving me crazy."

His tongue peeked out the corner of his mouth, doing nothing to disguise his smile. "That's the idea."

Time passed in a haze. He asked her where she went to college, about her hobbies and what books she liked to read, all while continuing that slow torture under her dress, those fingers inches from where she needed them to be. It was maddening. It was frustrating.

It was exhilarating.

By the time she was done mumbling about *The Walking Dead* graphic novels and how they were better than the TV show, because Lori was less annoying on paper, their food had arrived.

And she was a quivering mess.

Her food smelled amazing, which took her mind off the situation down below for about five minutes.

Until Austin's fingers curled, pushing her panties to the side, and then a finger dipped into her folds. She could feel how slick she was, and the only indication Austin made that he was as turned on as she was a small catch in his breath.

He picked up his fork with his left hand, and then paused to look at her. He took that moment to slip a finger inside of her. She gasped, and he blinked innocently. "Are you going to eat?"

She squeaked.

"Marley?" His voice was full of false concern.

She took a deep breath and picked up her knife to cut her chicken. It was in a bath of some sort of white wine sauce. The knife slipped out of her hand and clattered when he pumped his finger once.

"Careful, there," he admonished.

She wanted to hit him.

Instead she picked up her knife and tried again.

After a bite of chicken, that she admitted was heavenly, she found her voice, even though Austin had added a second finger and was slowly pumping them in and out of her. "I didn't realize you were left-handed."

He forked a mussel into his mouth, chewed, and swallowed. "I'm not."

She frowned and tried to remember if she'd seen him write. "But you're eating with your left hand."

He pressed down with the heel of his palm, right on her clit. She pulled her lips between her teeth and bit down. "That's because my right hand is busy with something a lot more important." He licked the tines of his fork. "And more delicious, if I remember."

"Fuck," she swore under her breath as he swirled the palm of his hand in time with his pumping fingers.

He twirled some noodles with his fork. "I'm actually ambidextrous."

She ran her tongue over her teeth. Of course he was.

"I used my left hand predominantly before I entered school." He set down his fork and flexed his left hand. "But then in kindergarten, I saw all the other kids using their right hand, and I began using my right hand." He flexed his fingers, then, twisted them deeper inside of her. "So I'm pretty good with both."

"I'd say you are," she said breathlessly, shoving another forkful of chicken into her mouth. "Lucky me."

One corner of his mouth tipped up and dark lashes fell over his beautiful eyes as he blinked slowly. "Lucky you."

His palm pressed over her clit again, sending sparks of pleasure down her legs. "Austin," she whispered. "Not sure how much more I can take."

He took a sip of his wine. "Just wait for dessert."

She ate the rest of her meal in silence, Austin's fingers doing delicious things between her legs. The waiter took their empty plates away and Austin ordered dessert. Marley was thankful she didn't have to talk. While they waited, he picked up her left leg and swung it over his thigh. She was stretched open now, completely bared under the table. She braced herself on the booth with one hand, and grasped Austin's wrist with the other. He was looking down, at his hand disappearing under her skirt.

"I'm going to smell you on my skin for weeks," he said softly, gaze still on his hand.

Marley squirmed and gripped his wrist tighter.

"I'm going to keep these panties, too. Maybe jerk off with them wrapped around my cock, imagining it's your lips."

His mouth. God, it could bring a nun to sin.

She turned to him, staring at his parted lips. "Kiss me."

He jerked his head up. "What?"

She rolled her hips. "When you picked me up, you didn't kiss me."

He blinked, like the thought hadn't occurred to him. "I—"

She smiled. "Just kiss me, Austin."

He reached out and clutched her neck, bringing her

face closer until their lips were an inch apart. She could feel his breath on her lips, spicy from his food. "Is this what you want?"

His fingers were working harder now, in and out. She could hear how wet she was. The whole situation was debauched and glorious. She was at his mercy, pinned in his booth, his fingers inside of her, his hand gripping her neck.

"Yes," she breathed. "I want you."

He pressed their lips together fiercely, his lips immediately opening, his tongue thrusting into her mouth, not even asking, but taking.

She arched her back and began working her hips, seeking, wanting that release as he fucked her with his fingers and his tongue at the same time. In that moment she was his. He completely owned her. And she loved it.

The release was starting. She could feel it in her spine, in every limb, every damn appendage. She heard herself whimper into his mouth, and her hips pumped harder.

"Can you come before the waiter brings our dessert?" he said against her lips, his fingers working harder.

She hadn't thought of that. God, the waiter would be able to see all over her face, in the positions of their bodies, what Austin was doing to her.

"He could come back any minute." Austin whispered. "He'd see you, eyes glazed with lust, riding my hand."

She was so close. So close. "Austin…"

"Only I get to see you like this. Come, my Evelyn."

She shoved her face into his neck and bit down on his skin to muffle her cries as the orgasm ripped through her. He worked her the whole time, with those fingers and that hand, extended her orgasm until she was wrung out and weak.

He withdrew his fingers, leaving her empty, and she felt the loss of them keenly. She shuddered against him and unlocked her jaw. But she didn't raise her head.

A hand sifted through her hair, lips brushed her temple.

"So beautiful." The words were whispered into her ear. "So perfect."

She breathed into his neck, trusting that he'd take care of everything. That he'd take care of her. He murmured words to her, his voice a low croon, and she melted into his lap. This wasn't just about sex anymore. Not with the way he took care of her and soothed her ragged nerves after the week she had.

She wanted to ask him how it was for him. She wanted to ask him if his heart was on the line at all. But that would come later. For now, she rested her weary bones.

When their dessert came, she didn't even look at it. And Austin asked for the check right away.

Chapter Ten

She was boneless when Austin led her to his car in the darkened parking lot. She almost took off her heels and walked barefoot, but she didn't want to cut her feet on broken glass or something. That would have ended what was the best date of her life on a sour note.

She needed to get herself together and find a second wind. Because the night was far from over. She'd been good, very good. And Austin had promised a reward.

They'd sat in the booth waiting for a check and Austin hadn't touched her other than a couple of caresses on her hand. She thought she'd done something wrong, but then he explained that he needed to calm down or he'd make a scene when they walked out of the restaurant. She'd glanced at his pants, saw the thick ridge straining against the zipper, and shut her mouth.

He was more demonstrative as he helped her into the car, leaning down to press a kiss to her temple before shutting the door.

When he started the car, she closed her eyes.

"You're not going to fall asleep on me, are you?" he asked.

She made exaggerated snoring noises.

There was a pause, and then he started laughing. She opened her eyes and rolled her head on the headrest to look at him. "I like your laugh."

He glanced at her, the streetlights cutting over his face, his normally tense expression now softened. She wondered if it was the result of the wine, her, or a little of both.

"You do?" he said. "Well, you often make me laugh."

Those words sent a warm curl into her belly. "I need to stay on top of my game. Come up with new material."

He laughed softly. "I don't doubt your talent."

When they pulled into the parking lot of her apartment complex, she pointed to the guest parking spots. His car looked odd, mixed with the nineties models that populated the lot.

She wondered if he'd assume he was invited up to her apartment. When he threw the car into park, he didn't turn off the engine, but turned to look at her. Only one eye was visible in a shaft of light—the rest of his face was in shadow. That eye was on her, assessing.

She unlocked her seat belt and opened her door. Over her shoulder she said, "Well, are you coming?"

He raised his eyebrows.

She lowered a heel to the ground. "You promised me something." She stood up with a smile on her face and closed the car door behind her. She hadn't had a man in her apartment other than Chad in…well, way too long. She'd placed so much emphasis on her career, and while it still meant the world to her, she had never felt alive like she did with Austin. Video games had been her escape for so long, a way to operate in a carefully controlled world. She lived for it. But that was nothing compared to her reaction in Austin's presence, his strong palm on her neck.

Marley walked to her apartment without looking behind her. She heard a car door shut, a beep of the locks, and then footfalls. Austin didn't run to catch up; he trailed her by about five feet, his shoes clacking on the staircase as they made their ascent to the third floor.

A zing shot through her. This was like a hunt, and she was his prey. God, how she wanted to be his prey, like a mouse in his talons.

This was all she needed, this game. She was turned on all over again, the area between her legs slick. She wanted more than his mouth and his fingers. She wanted that cock he'd promised, sliding into her, slow and tortuous, then hot and pounding until they both collapsed from exhaustion.

Her skin heated, her clothes too tight, constricting. She scratched under her neckline and turned to look at Austin over her shoulder.

His eyes were on her, the pale irises catching the light in the stairwell. She walked faster, as much as she could in her heels, and his steps picked up.

It was a game, she knew that. But she liked it, feeling like he was chasing her, that anticipation of his hands on her.

She reached her apartment door and pulled her keys out of her purse. His footsteps stopped and his shadow fell over her door.

She managed to get the keys in the lock and then his

body was there, crowding her inside. The door slammed shut behind her and then her back was against the door, his heat at her front.

He palmed the door on either side of her head and ran his nose up the cord on the side of her neck. "You liked that, didn't you? Me chasing you."

She didn't bother answering. He knew her body so well.

He took a hand off the door and settled it at her throat. She brought her hands up and clutched his forearm. He stared at her fingers, where they wrapped around his wrists, nails digging into his skin.

His eyes darkened. "What else does my Evelyn fantasize about?"

Him. He was the subject of her fantasies. She'd never touched herself as much as she had since she met him.

"Tell me," he whispered.

She swallowed. "Me…bent over the kitchen table, my skirt around my waist and…my ass red because you spanked me."

His eyes fluttered closed and when he opened them again, he seemed to have trouble focusing. When he spoke again, his voice was husky. "What else?"

"Me, on my knees in the shower. Your cock in my mouth. Your fingers twisted in my wet hair."

"Christ," he swore under his breath. He stepped closer now, and his hardness brushed against her hip.

She swallowed. "You, fucking me from behind, like that… GIF. Remember?"

His lips were parted, harsh breaths coming from between them. "Of course I fucking remember."

She smiled. His eyes watched her mouth.

And then his lips slammed down on hers as he pressed a thigh between her legs. She arched her back and hips off of the wall as he devoured her, that strong hand on her throat keeping her head in place.

She didn't know what picture she made as she ground herself onto his thigh. She didn't care. Because she wanted him...needed him. But he kept his hips far enough away that she couldn't feel what she wanted to feel.

"Austin," she moaned into his mouth.

He pulled away, his lips wet and swollen. He let go of her throat and stepped back, his gaze trailing down her body and back again. "Bedroom."

Marley made to step out of her heels but he shook his head. "Leave those on."

She rolled her lips between her teeth and ducked her head. She walked past him, his intense gaze on her skin like a brand.

He followed her, his steps hard and purposeful. There was that hunted feeling again, the prickle on the back of her neck echoing between her legs.

When they reached her bedroom, she flicked on the light beside her bed and turned to face Austin. He was looking around the room, and when he found her floor length mirror on her wall by her closet, he smiled.

It was an evil smile.

She liked it.

"Go stand in front of the mirror," he directed, his voice low.

She did as she was told.

"Take off your dress," he murmured softly.

The zipper was low, so she could reach it herself. She

watched him in the mirror, watching her, as she zipped it down her back to the top of her ass. She let it pool at her feet, then stepped out of it and kicked it aside. She stood in front of the mirror now, in her heels, thigh-highs, garter belt, thong, and bra. All black lace.

Just like the GIF. She'd planned that.

Her lips were swollen and her hair was a mess of curls. She had never been a woman to wax on about her appearance in any way. But right now…she felt beautiful, sexy. Wanton.

Movement in the mirror caught her attention. Behind her, Austin took off his suit jacket and folded it neatly, setting it on the bench at the end of her bed. Then he slipped out his cufflinks and set those on her dresser. He rolled up his sleeves to his elbows and unbuttoned his shirt, baring his chest underneath.

Then he stepped out of his shoes and peeled off his socks, stuffing them inside his shoes. Everything was done slowly, meticulously. Probably all meant to drive her crazy and that was okay. It sure as hell *was* driving her crazy.

Only then, when he was barefoot, dress shirt unbuttoned, bulge in his pants, did he meet her gaze in the mirror.

He walked toward her slowly. "How could you think I'd forget that GIF, Marley?"

She swallowed and didn't answer. He stopped behind her and lowered his eyes. A palm skimmed the top of her bare ass. Her eyes fell shut, then slammed back open as he smacked the top of one ass cheek, and then the other. Each crack was loud in the silent room, startling her. She stumbled on her heels and almost fell, but Austin grabbed her around the throat and hauled her back against his body.

With his other hand, he soothed the sting of his slaps.
The calluses on his fingers rasped over her skin and she
moaned. He watched her in the mirror. "One day, I'll put
you over my knee"—he smirked—"or the kitchen table, and
do that again."

She squirmed.

"Would you like that?"

She gulped against his hand. "Yes."

Keeping his one hand at her throat, he pulled down the
cups of her bra, so her breasts swung free. He slapped the
tips lightly, which tightened her nipples and forced another
groan from her throat.

"Are you watching yourself, Marley?" he asked, his
moist breath coating her neck. "Are you watching as I enjoy
what's mine?"

She honestly considered shoving her fingers in her
panties and rubbing her clit until she came. Jesus, his voice.
It was like honey. "Yes, I'm watching."

He stepped closer, and she could feel his erection at the
top of her ass. He ran the back of his fingers down her stomach and then traced the line of her thong below her belly
button. "This is what you want, right? This is what you saw
on your computer. A man's hand at your throat? His hand
down your panties?"

Not just any man, she wanted to say. *You*. Before she
met Austin, every time she fantasized about that, it had been
with a faceless man. It had been all about her, her pleasure.
But now, she knew only Austin would do in this scenario.
And she wanted to please him.

Instead of saying that, all she did was nod.

His fingers dipped into her thong and then cupped her,

his middle finger slipping into her slit. She was still wet from before, still so sensitive. He pulled on her throat, squeezing, so she had to lean back on his shoulder and part her lips to get air. She trusted him, though, to make sure this was safe, to make sure this was good for her. And God it was good. It was amazing. It was perfect, his hand at her throat, squeezing, owning, possessing, while his fingers worked magic below in her wetness.

"Look at yourself," he rasped, face beside hers.

She opened her eyes to watch his hand go in and out, in and out of her thong.

"I've never seen anything more beautiful, Marley," he said.

She blinked her eyes as the sting of tears began. "Me either."

His tongue ran along the shell of her ear. "I promised you something if you were good. And oh, my Evelyn, you've been so good."

Marley closed her eyes as he sucked her earlobe into his mouth.

"Do you want my cock, sweetheart?"

"Yes," she gasped.

"In front of this mirror? You bent over, so you can watch as I fuck you?"

"Jesus." She could already see it—her braced against the mirror, his hands on her hips, his eyes watching where he plunged his cock in and out of her.

Oh God, she wanted that.

"That's what Marley wants," he murmured in her ear.

"H-How do you know?"

"I can see it in your face."

He stepped away from her, his hand falling from her throat, his fingers slipping out of her underwear. She managed to stay on her feet by bracing her hands on the mirror in front of her. He unclasped her bra and slipped it down her arms, and then he helped her step out of her thong. He told her to stay in her garter belt, thigh-highs, and heels. She didn't object.

He flicked open the button on his pants and pulled down his zipper. She watched as he pulled out his cock, thick and hard, jutting from a base of curly dark hair. He was mostly clothed and she was mostly...not.

And it was so hot.

He tore open a condom wrapper he pulled from his pocket, then slid the condom down his length. He stood square behind her, stroking his cock a couple of times, his gaze on her ass.

"Bend over more. Stick out your ass for me, sweetheart."

She did, bracing her forearms on the mirror, tilting her ass up so he could see her. On display. His for the taking.

Sure it was a game, but he was controlling it. And she was happy about that. He was quite good at the controls, which buttons to press and in what order. At least, all her buttons.

He stepped closer and gripped her hip. He ran the tip of his cock through her wetness, and she whimpered when he ran it over her clit.

His face was intense, heated. The only indication she had that he'd had enough foreplay was a slight widening of his stance. Because then he gripped her hips and slammed into her.

She cried out, almost hitting her forehead on the mirror.

She flexed her arms, bracing herself more solidly. Then a hand wrapped in the curls at her neck, pulling her head back. "Watch us," he said hoarsely.

That command was what she needed as he pulled out to the tip and plunged back in, then out. His hips slammed into her ass and she arched her back. His balls slapped against her as he began a steady rhythm. His eyes were glued to their connection, watching himself enter her body again and again.

She watched as her breasts jolted beneath her, her lips opened on a silent cry. Her knees shook in her heels. And despite his hold on her hip and hair, she was flying. Her brain shut off and soared because there was only pleasure, and a little bit of pain. And Austin. And *them*. This moment as their bodies joined.

"Oh God," she whispered, because she could feel her orgasm building but she needed more. She couldn't let go of the mirror or she'd fall. His eyes shot to hers and he watched her face in the mirror.

While still connected, he pulled her up, clutching her throat with one hand, his other dipping down, those fingers swirling over her clit. With her in her heels, their heights matched up so he could continue pumping in and out of her. His breath panted into her ear, the slick skin of his chest was hot on her back.

His fingers worked magic in tandem with his cock, and she was close, oh so close. If his stuttering rhythm was any indication, he was too.

He kept his gaze locked on hers as he lowered his head and sucked on her neck, and that added bit of pressure, along with a squeeze to her throat, was all she needed to send her over the edge. She cried out as she came. And came. And came. On his fingers, on his cock. The spasms echoed all over her body.

This was it. This was the moment where she let go, where she flew, where she lived. Where nothing was her responsibility but pleasure—for herself and for Austin—and when they were together, it was like second nature.

This was when she was alive. And this was what she'd been missing.

She clutched his hips as they faltered behind her, and then he shoved his face into her neck and groaned against her skin. He pulsed inside of her, and she let her eyes close as he found his release.

She breathed deeply, registering that her feet were killing her and her legs were noodles.

Austin raised his head off of her neck, and looked at her in the mirror. Their gazes met and held. His one hand was on the top of her chest, the other splayed along her belly. He closed his fingers and then opened them again, pressing them into her skin. She raised an arm weakly and curled it around his head, sifting through his hair.

He blinked slowly, like he'd been drugged. "You're incredible."

She smiled. "You're pretty okay, yourself."

One corner of his mouth curled up. He stepped back slowly, separating himself from her, and she wondered if that felt as wrong for him as it did for her.

He picked her up with an arm at her back and one under her knees. He took two steps and laid her down on the bed. She watched as he slipped off her heels and rolled down her thigh-highs and garter belt. Then he pressed a kiss to her hip.

"I'll be right back."

She nodded and watched as he walked into her bathroom.

The toiled flushed, the sink ran. And then he walked back in the room, sans pants. Sans anything. His hair was mussed from her fingers and his chest was damp from sweat. The muscles in his thighs bulged with each step and she made a mental note to bite one later.

"Do you sleep naked?" she asked.

He paused, eyes on her, with an intense expression on his face. She opened her mouth to ask him what he was thinking, but then he shook his head, and his face relaxed. He closed the distance to the bed and put a knee to the mattress. He lifted up the comforter, helping her scramble underneath it then sliding in beside her. He wrapped an arm around her waist. "I do now."

She reached out and cupped his cheek, rubbing her thumb over the stubble on his jaw. Then she pressed a kiss to his lips. "Thank you for a wonderful date."

His eyes were half-closed. "It wasn't a comic convention but I hope it was sufficient."

She laughed. "Quite sufficient."

He tucked her into his side. "Good, now go to sleep and we can do some more sufficient things tomorrow morning."

She nestled into his chest, her fingers slipping down his ribs to rest on his hip. "I'd like that."

He kissed the top of her head, and she pressed closer, listening to the steady rhythm of his heart. She'd get up in a minute and wash her face and brush her teeth. But for now, she didn't want to move.

Chapter Eleven

Fingers traced over his skin in small circles, swirling the short hair on his chest. At first his body tensed, and those fingers paused. He willed himself to relax his muscles, one by one. Because he remembered now where he was — in Marley's bed, her hands on him, her hair tickling his shoulder.

It was a weird sensation to wake up next to anyone. He hadn't done it since…college maybe, and that had probably been when he lived with Grant. Waking up next to a warm body was unfamiliar, but he'd made the decision last night. His first instinct had been to put on his clothes and go home, but then he'd seen Marley in her bed, naked, with a flushed face and small smile. And he hadn't wanted to leave. He wanted to stay in her presence.

Now, as her hand lowered to the furred ridges of his abs, he knew he'd made the right call. One lone finger traced the trail leading down to his cock. Which was also awake. Very awake.

Her weight beside him shifted, and he still kept his eyes closed as the sheet shifted from around his hips. Cool air hit his cock and balls.

Then those fingers wrapped around his shaft and the head was engulfed in a tight, suctioning heat.

He opened his eyes then on a groan to the sight of Marley between his legs. Her hair was a riot of curls, and the morning sun streaking through the curtains glinted off the highlights of red in the strands. Her lips pulled off of his cock, and she looked at him from under her lashes.

She stuck her tongue out and swirled it once around the head, then smirked. He shoved a pillow under his head so he could see better, then reached down, his thumb at the corner of her mouth, hand on her chin. "Do that again."

She lost her smirk at his command, and her eyes glazed. Fuck, she was perfect. One order from him and he bet anything she was getting wet. She stuck out her tongue and swirled it again, slower this time.

"Take it in your mouth now. Suck me."

Her eyes fell closed as she wrapped those lips around his cock and descended on a moan.

"Look at me."

Her eyes popped open, then fell to half mast. Her ass was in the air as she kneeled between his legs and her hips pumped. "Are you touching yourself?"

She made a sound around his cock and then her hips stopped moving.

"That's what I thought. I want to see both of your hands while you suck me. Trust me to take care of you."

She brought her one hand in sight and gripped his

thigh, while her other hand gripped the base of his shaft. He reached around and tangled his fingers in her hair. "Go on. I want to come in that mouth. I want to see those lips wet with me."

She worked him harder, humming a little under her breath. The vibration traveled down his shaft, into his balls, and down his legs.

His cock disappeared between her lips, her cheeks hollowing as she took him inside her mouth, and he knew she was his oasis. She was life in the desert that had been his existence.

The orgasm started in his spine, rolling throughout his body. He squeezed her hair once in warning, but she didn't pull off. She kept working him as he arched his back and came into her mouth. The orgasm was slow moving but it seemed to go on forever, each aftershock as intense as the last. By the time he was finished, he was wrung out and boneless. She took what he had, sucking him until he let go of her hair. Then she let his shaft slip from her mouth. He lay flat on his back, staring at the ceiling.

She crawled up his body and collapsed on top of him. He only had the energy to wrap an arm around her shoulders.

"Good morning," she said, her breath hot on his skin.

"Jesus."

"Actually, it's Marley."

He groaned. "I think you might kill me."

She propped herself up on his chest. "Can't keep up with me, old man?"

He narrowed his eyes. "I'm not that much older than you."

She raised an eyebrow.

Well, shit, how old was she? "Am I?"

She laughed. "I'm twenty-seven."

"Thirty-two, so you can't call me old man unless there's at least a decade between us." She pressed her lips together and it was his turn to raise an eyebrow. "Did an old man give you two orgasms last night?"

She blushed and tucked her head into his neck.

He laughed and ran a hand up her spine. "That's what I thought."

She squirmed on top of him and mumbled something into his neck.

"What?"

She raised her head. "I think you're forgetting something this morning."

He frowned and tapped his finger on his lips. "No, I definitely don't think so."

She squirmed again. "Austin…"

He reached down, slipping his hand over her ass then dipping between her legs. And hell yeah, she was wet.

He circled her entrance and she squirmed more, pushing against his fingers. He pulled his hand back and smacked her ass. She yelped and then threw back her head and laughed, her hair whipping him in the face.

He grinned. "How about this? I make us breakfast, then I'll come back and take my time with you."

She cupped his face and rubbed her thumb over his lips. Her face softened. "I like when you smile."

He squeezed her hip. "Well, I seem to do it a lot around you."

Her gaze met his. "I'm glad."

He didn't say anything else. He didn't want to move,

really. Marley's weight and heat were pressed into him, her legs straddling one of his. He could have lain there forever staring into her eyes. But he was hungry.

He gently rolled her off of him and she fell onto the bed on her back, her curls in a mass around her head. She smiled up at him and he pressed a kiss between her breasts. "I'm going to go hunt around your kitchen for breakfast."

"I can come out, ya know." She smacked him lightly on the arm.

He shook his head. "Nope, you stay in bed."

"Yes, sir," she said sternly.

He stood at the end of the bed and stretched. "Don't get fresh."

She stuck out her tongue at him.

Austin tugged on his boxer briefs and made his way out to the kitchen. Marley seemed to have a lot of refrigerated cookie dough and not much else. He managed to scrounge up some eggs, bread for toast, and strawberries that were about a day away from going bad.

After making the coffee, he popped the bread in the toaster and cracked some eggs into a pan to scramble. While the eggs were cooking, he sliced up the strawberries.

He'd been cooking for himself since he was tall enough to reach the knobs on the stove. His dad worked odd hours and even when he was home, preferred takeout. Austin became quite adept at throwing an odd assortment of ingredients together—whatever they had on hand or was on sale at the store—into something quite edible. He still preferred to cook. Although he preferred his kitchen at his house. He'd have to take Marley there sometime and cook her dinner.

The thought of bringing Marley to his house rolled

around in his brain and settled into his gut.

A woman. At his place.

But Marley wasn't any woman. She was Marley, and after last night, it was clear that this was getting big, really big. This wasn't just about fulfilling Marley's fantasies anymore, was it? That was what he'd been telling himself, that this was all for her, but it was for him, too. That was clear now.

He still hadn't told her about the biggest parts of his life. He'd let this go on and now there was no easy separation, no way to get out of this without her finding out the truth.

He paused, his knife mid-slice on a strawberry. If he sold *Gamers*, though, before he told her, maybe it would lessen the blow. And then he'd no longer be involved in her job in any way. She'd probably still throw things and yell at him, but there could be forgiveness. He hoped.

Because Marley was worth holding on to. And he was a selfish bastard for wanting to keep her.

He dropped the strawberries into a bowl and began to scramble the eggs.

The date had been great, better than great. Everything about Marley turned him on, from her humor, to her body, to the way she responded to him, with her parted lips and red cheeks.

The way she trusted him. She deserved some of that trust back. But damn, it was hard for Austin to do that. As soon as he trusted people, let them in, they had the power to hurt him. And Marley… she could crush him, he knew. She had more power than she thought. Maybe all of it.

He slipped the finished eggs onto two plates, found a tray in a lower cabinet, and placed everything—along with two coffees—on it.

When he walked back into the bedroom with the loaded tray, Marley was on the bed, reading glasses perched on her nose, silk robe hanging loosely on her shoulders.

The robe was blue silk.

He was hard again already.

She looked up from the ereader in her hands then set it aside on her nightstand, along with the glasses. She smiled when she saw the food. "Wow, I'm really impressed."

He shrugged. A monkey could make scrambled eggs.

"I can't make scrambled eggs," Marley muttered, gaze on the tray. "I always manage to burn them."

He didn't voice his monkey-chef opinion.

He motioned for her to sit back against the pillows on the headboard, then handed her a plate of eggs with a side of strawberries and her steaming cup of coffee. She set her mug on her nightstand and shoved a forkful of scrambled eggs into her mouth. She moaned around the bite.

He raised an eyebrow. "Are they satisfactory?"

She nodded and forked in another bite. "Could use ketchup though," she mumbled, her mouth full.

Despite her manners, she made a beautiful picture. Cross-legged on her bed, hair wild, face fresh of makeup. Her robe gapped at the top, so he saw the top swell of a breast. He looked away and focused on his food.

"So," he stabbed a strawberry and put it in his mouth. "What changed your mind? About us? I was surprised when I got that email from you."

She took a sip of her coffee. "Well, I realized I'd denied myself for a lot of years. I'd worked really hard, and I don't regret it. But you…" She licked her lips and blushed. "You make me feel a way I'm not sure I've ever felt." Her eyes darted up to meet his, widening a little. "I mean, I know we just had one date, I'm not—"

He held a hand up to stop her. "I didn't take you out with the intention of only one date. And I'd say it's going pretty well, right?"

Her lips stretched into a smile. "Yeah, I would say so. Well, anyway, I decided I was just being paranoid. You're not a coworker, and there are no rules against that anyway. And while you might be a distraction, I'm a big girl, and I can handle it."

The weight of his lie sat in his stomach along with his eggs and coffee. He should tell her, come clean.

He looked down at his plate and picked at a large chunk of egg. "What's your background before you were hired at *Gamers*?" He had no involvement in the hiring of the employees, so he'd never seen her résumé.

She talked about her journalism days and told a funny story about covering a senior home's Olympics competition. Marley was engaging when she talked, her voice full of inflection, her hands flying as she demonstrated an event.

"So. I don't know much about you," she said, when she was finished talking.

He set his fork on his plate and leaned back against the pillows on the headboard, feet crossed at the ankles. "No, I guess you don't."

She watched him, her gaze on his face. "I get the sense you're private."

He pressed his lips together. "That sense would be absolutely correct."

She blinked, and he didn't miss the disappointment that flashed over her face.

This hurt, a lot. Opening up wasn't something he did. It felt unnatural. He'd learned at a young age how to hide the fact that his family didn't have a lot of money so he wasn't teased at school. It was embarrassing if other people found out how little his father paid attention to him.

But Grant was right. His need to keep everyone out was turning him into a lonely man, and it wasn't comforting anymore.

So he took a deep breath and ignored the barbs that accompanied the words as they left his mouth. As he spoke, he stared at the blank screen of the TV on Marley's dresser. "My…uh…mother left shortly after I was born. I'm not sure where she is. Or if she's alive. So my father raised me. We didn't have a lot of money and he was gone a lot, working odd hours as a shift supervisor at a warehouse."

He waved his hand toward his plate. "It's why I can cook. I earned an academic scholarship to attend MIT, and for the rest of my tuition I took out loans. It was rough. I…" He glanced at Marley now. Her attention was rapt. "I made some investments that paid off."

He didn't mention one of those investments was making and selling *Aric's Revenge* to a large software developer. Or starting *Gamers*. "And it was fine, until I found out my father was taking money from me. He'd had access to my accounts and I'd been helping him out but he…well, I guess he thought I should be helping him more. But he didn't ask, he just took, and I didn't realize until my tuition check bounced."

"Oh, Austin," Marley said, her voice not full of sympathy, really, but anger. For him.

"So, I cut him off. I was twenty-one and I thought I was hot shit. We didn't speak after that. He was stubborn as hell, and I inherited that. He died of pancreatic cancer a couple of years ago. I hadn't spoken to him since college."

She shifted closer now, and slipped her hand into his. "I'm really sorry."

He blew out a breath, and with it came a chuckle, which turned into a full on fit of laughter. Marley stared at him like he was crazy. He probably was a little crazy. He shook his head. "I'm sorry, I just…I thought that was going to be a lot harder than it was. To say all that. To open up. I don't even talk to my best friend about it much but I…" He pulled her closer until she was pressed against his side. He cupped her cheek. "I wanted to give you something back, for all you've given me, so there you go."

He hadn't given her everything, but damn, this was new. Baby steps.

She smiled and leaned into his touch. "Thank you for that. For giving that to me. And for what it's worth, I'm sorry that things happened the way they did for you and your father."

He rubbed a thumb over her bottom lip. "Yeah, well, it is what it is."

With a kiss to her forehead, he rolled off the bed and grabbed their plates. "I'll do the dishes and be right back."

She stretched. "This is ridiculous. I've been a bum. I can do the dishes."

"Just relax." He was already walking out the door of the bedroom.

After he loaded the dishwasher and cleaned up from breakfast, he made his way back to the bedroom. He heard the familiar soundtrack of *Aric's Revenge* and stopped in the hallway. He laid a hand on the wall and closed his eyes. He knew he was going to have to tell her. And he would. One day. But he'd done enough sharing for now, and he'd rather spend the rest of their time today with his mouth attached to various parts of her body.

He walked in and spotted her propped against the headboard, knees bent, eyes on the TV. She looked up. "Oh hey, sorry. I beat this game way back when it came out but the movie made me nostalgic so I'm playing it again." She pressed the button to save her game.

He put a knee to the bed and pushed her forward so he could sit behind her, then he rested her back against his chest. "You don't have to stop." He ran his fingers up and down her thighs.

"But—"

He spread her legs gently, hooking her knees over his thighs, so she was open in front of him, displayed for him.

"Austin," she whispered, almost dropping the controller.

He pressed a kiss to her neck. "Keep playing."

He untied her robe, and the sound of the silk slipping against itself sent a shot of pleasure right to his cock where it rested against her lower back.

She squirmed, and he flicked his eyes to the screen. Aric ran into a wall and she cursed under her breath. He smiled and spread the edges of her robe apart.

Her breasts rose and fell with her breaths. Her nipples were red and hard. He held one breast in each hand, rubbing his thumbs over the buds.

"I-I can't—"

"Aric has to get into the castle," he murmured. "You can't stop playing now."

She made a sound in the back of her throat, and he

smiled into her neck. He loved her breasts. They were high and full. No matter what she wore, the swells under her clothes never ceased to draw his attention.

Her stomach tensed as his one hand left a breast and continued downward. On the TV, Aric was searching the stone walls for a way inside the castle.

He slipped a hand down further, into the small bit of pubic hair she kept neatly trimmed. She whimpered and accidentally slashed Aric's sword against the rocks.

"Now now," he said, dipping lower to tap lightly on her clit. "Can't go hacking away without finding the right spot first. The way inside."

"Jesus," she swore, her hands trembling as they held the remote.

He placed his lips at her ear as she continued around the back of the castle, feeling the walls for loose stones. "It can be tricky. Not everyone can find it. Do you know where it is?"

She licked her lips and opened her mouth. No sound came out at first, and when her voice finally did, it was in a rush. "Between the two columns at the far left corner."

He dipped lower into her folds, taking her wetness and spreading it around.

"Very good," he said. "But you can't just barge in, right? You have to work the stones free gently."

She was breathing hard now, her breasts heaving. Her legs clenched around his. The buttons on the remote clicked as Marley entered in a combination. On the screen, Aric took the hilt of his sword and began to tap away at a stone. Dust began to seep out, falling at his booted feet. Austin remembered designing that area of the wall. The weak stone was only noticeable by a small clump of slightly darker gray pixels right in the center.

"There you go," Austin said, swirling Marley's clit. Her hips began to rock. "Take your time. There's no rush."

Marley swallowed and a bead of sweat dripped down her neck. Austin licked it up.

He lowered his hand, circling the wetness around her entrance as the dust built up a small pile at Aric's feet. The stone began to push into the wall.

"A little bit more," Austin said.

Marley's arms were coated in goose bumps, as she jammed her thumb over and over again on the button at the top of the controller. Aric continued to slam the hilt of his sword on the stone.

Then the telltale sound of grinding as the stone slid inside, and Austin slid his finger home.

She gasped and dropped the controller, gripping Austin's wrist as he worked her with his fingers. "Oh my God," she moaned, her hips rocking harder.

He watched his hand moving between the silk edges of her robe. "So beautiful, Marley. Fuck, I've never seen anything like it."

"More," she pleaded.

He smiled and nodded to the controller between her legs. "Pick it up."

"Aussssstin."

"Pick it up. You know Bauer's guards will be coming any minute. Aric has to take them out."

"You gotta be kidding me right now," she said through gritted teeth, her fingernails digging into his wrist.

He grinned harder, liking the pain, and stilled his fingers.

"Nope. You can't come until you reach Bauer's throne and defeat him."

"I hate you."

"No, you don't."

She growled under her breath. Then to Austin's complete satisfaction, she picked up the controller and readied Aric's sword for the imminent attack.

Austin's cock was hard and aching where it rested at her back, and two of his fingers were sunk deep inside of her while she played a video game *he* developed. He wished he could go back in time and tell his awkward, dorky, thirteen-year-old self to hang in there because life sure as hell got a whole lot better.

Bauer was the King who held Evelyn hostage. He was a sadistic bastard who held a grudge over Aric's family. And right now, his guards were about to discover Aric.

This was close to the end of the game, where Aric made the choice to turn away from seeking revenge on Bauer by taking his wife by force, and instead forges a rescue operation for Evelyn.

Austin waited, counting down the seconds, based on the flickering light of the hallway sconce, to when the guards would discover Aric walking down the back hallways of the castle.

3...2...1...

A set of three guards came around the corner, bracing once they spotted Aric. Before the middle guard could alert more guards, Marley cut Aric's sword in a downward arc, cleanly taking his head off. Then she stabbed the other in the side, right where there was a gap in his armor. She crouched and swung Aric's leg out, taking the third man down, then stuck the sword into his neck.

All three men were dispatched before they could alert more guards.

Austin was impressed.

He wiggled his fingers and her chest hitched.

"You're a bastard," she muttered.

"You're a hell of a player."

She eyed him over her shoulder, a smirk on her mouth. She ground her ass back into his cock and now it was his turn to catch his breath. She winked. "I'm no amateur."

"I see that."

She continued toward the center of the castle, where Austin knew the throne room was. A legend map was optional, but he noticed Marley didn't bother pulling it up on the screen. He smiled.

He began to move his fingers again as she drew closer to Bauer, wanting to see how well she played while distracted. Her hips were moving, almost involuntary, like dancing to the beat of a song, but instead riding his fingers.

He pressed a kiss to her shoulder as the sounds of the throne room grew louder—the voices, clanging of swords, booted footsteps.

Aric burst into the room with a roar, taking out the weakest guards first. Marley breathed heavy as Aric's sword flashed in the room, taking down as many enemies as she could. Austin moved his fingers, curling them inside of her and she groaned, her eyelids closing before popping back open. Aric fell against a wall and took a hit to his hip.

He rose and began fighting again but Marley was more distracted now. Her arms shook and her fingers pressed wrong buttons.

The timer began to tick. Aric's anger level was sixty-seven percent, and if she could hold it, the dragons would come. That was the only way to beat this level.

He moved his fingers with the timer and counted into her ear. "One." He licked her earlobe. "Two." Marley moaned as he raked his teeth down her neck. "Three." He took his free hand and grabbed a condom he'd left on the nightstand the evening before. "Four." He ripped it open with his teeth and struggled one-handed to roll it down his incredibly hard cock. There was a moment of silence as both of them froze, like the moment before the tornado touches the ground. Before lightning strikes a tree. Before a wave crashes down.

"Five."

Large talons crashed through the ceiling of the castle's throne room and giant wings beat the air. The dragons were there, and they'd wreak their destruction until no one was left standing but Aric.

Austin took the controller from Marley and tossed it onto the pillows. He shoved her onto her back, and then he rammed home.

She cried out, thrashing below him, hissing out a "yesss" and raking her nails down his shoulders.

He went down to his forearms, gripping her hair with his fingers, holding her head in place as he pounded into her, unable to stop himself or tone down his intensity.

She stared up at him, her eyes wide, her mouth open, pure pleasure etched in every line of her face. Her thighs gripped him like a vice and her heels dug into his ass, urging him on.

She squeezed her eyes shut and when she opened them, tears leaked out of the corners. He wiped them away with his thumbs, and she made a small sound in her throat. Her fingers worked between them, and he knew when she started coming because her inner walls began to contract around him.

That was all he needed, as she cried out his name, for his own orgasm to knock into him with the force of that huge wave crashing to the ground. The lightning striking the tree. The tornado touching down.

He collapsed on top of her, his face shoved into her neck, while she wrapped her arms around him and held on tight as the last of his orgasm was wrung from his body and into hers.

Her fingers carded through his hair and curled around the strands at the nape of his neck. She pressed a kiss to his temple, and he squeezed his eyes shut. In a short matter of time, this woman had definitely found his weak points and snuck her way into his castle walls.

He thought about opening his mouth right there, telling her that he was technically kinda sorta her boss. That he also kinda sorta wrote code for the video game that she'd just played.

It wasn't the hesitancy to trust that kept his mouth shut this time. It was the timing. He didn't want to leave her body, her warm embrace. He didn't want to see those hazel eyes darken in anger.

He'd wait. He had a plan. He'd talk to Grant, maybe convince him to seek more offers. Once Austin sold *Gamers*, he'd tell her. And then he'd reveal his part in *Aric's Revenge* too. He could only hope that by then he'd have worn down the weak points in *her* walls enough for her to find it in her heart to forgive him.

He held her closer. "You did it. You won."

She rolled her head to the side, where the screen showed Aric in an empty throne room, surrounded by ashes and his dragons. "Oh, yeah, I won the game."

He shook his head. "I wasn't talking about the game."

She stared at him, her mouth open in an O, before she closed her lips and curved them into a smile. "Oh yeah? What else did I win?" She cupped his cheek, her thumb brushing his stubble.

"You won a grumpy IT guy with control issues."

She giggled, her body jerking under his. "Wow, it's like Christmas!"

He pressed a kiss to her lips. "Lucky you."

She was silent for a moment as her face softened. "Yeah, lucky me."

Chapter Twelve

Marley fussed with the flowers, rearranging them in the vase, checking the water levels. She had even spent time online, looking up each respective flower, so she muttered the names as she touched each petal, each leaf. "Lily. Dahlia. Viburnum."

"Mars, quit talking to your plants." Chad opened up her refrigerator and pulled out a beer. He screwed off the top and threw it in her sink.

She glared at him, fished it out of the basin, and tossed it in the trash. "You're just jealous you didn't get any flowers."

"I'm more jealous you got breakfast in bed." He raised an eyebrow and took a pull of his beer.

She'd told him about the date...well, most of it. She'd left out pretty important chunks, like how Austin had his hand up her skirt the entire dinner, and like how he'd edged her over a game of *Aric's Revenge*.

She shifted uncomfortably. She still couldn't think about

it without flushing.

"So what's the verdict? You going to see him again?" Chad asked.

Austin had left Sunday afternoon with a kiss on the cheek and a promise to call. He had called, too, every day. It was now Tuesday evening and she'd already talked to him as she drove home from work. He said he wanted to take her out again on Friday and she had tried not to sound too eager, when all she wanted to do was jump up and down. This could actually be something with a guy that turned her inside out. And more than that, she felt needed. She made him laugh, and smile, and he'd confided in her, which he was clearly not accustomed to doing.

She pushed the flowers closer to the window and turned to face Chad. She leaned back on the counter, grabbing the edges. "Yeah, actually, he asked me out again. Friday."

Chad placed his beer on the table and smiled. "That's great, I'm really happy for you."

She shuffled her feet, the ears flopping on her fuzzy bunny slippers. "He makes me feel beautiful. And sexy. And important." She raised her head. "Isn't that what we all dream about? To feel wanted and important, like we're making a difference in another person's life? Like we fulfill them in some way."

Chad cocked his head to the side and rotated his beer on the counter. "Yeah, I guess we all do."

"I don't know where this is going to go, but I'm willing to put in the work for it. I think he's worth it."

"And he's awesome in bed."

Marley blushed. Yeah, so she'd told her brother that much. "That's just icing on the cake. I genuinely like him."

"I think he seems like a good guy, Marley. I approve. You got over how weirded out you were about the job thing?"

She shrugged. "Yeah, I don't know what my malfunction was, but I realized that there's really no conflict of interest, no reason I can't see him. So once I got over my own neuroses, it's been fine."

"Anyone at the office know?"

She shook her head. "No reason for them to, and I think Austin is respecting me by staying away." She bit her lip. The other reason might be because he'd told her he couldn't look at the supply closet without getting hard. Oops.

Chad clapped his hands together. "So, while we wait for the pizza, let's talk about your interview."

Marley nodded, setting her game face. "Yes. So I know James and Grant like me already, but Owen told me there were a couple of other people interviewing like"—she coughed—"Sorrel." Another cough. "So, I need to make sure I show them everything I've done at *Gamers* and why I deserve the position."

"Do you think they'll talk to Owen?"

"I don't know. I hope so. Because I know he's rooting for me."

"Can you get him to make a statement about you or something?"

Marley wrinkled her nose. "It doesn't really work that way."

Chad's face fell. "Oh."

"You're helping, Chad, I swear you are."

He smiled again. "I actually have a lot of experience with interviews. I've done more of those than actual jobs."

Marley rolled her eyes. "Only you."

He opened his mouth, but the doorbell rang, cutting him off. He stuck his fists in the air. "Pizza!" Then he grabbed Marley's wallet off the counter and trotted to the front door. She glared as he handed over her cash, but didn't protest. She'd asked him to come over anyway. She didn't think about all the times he'd asked her to come over and still paid with her money.

Her phone rang and she saw it was James. She frowned, because it was almost seven at night. "Hello?"

"Marley." James' voice scratched over the line.

"Hey, James. You still at work?"

"No, no, but I wanted to call to give you as much notice as possible. I know we mentioned Thursday for your interview, but can we move it to tomorrow night, by any chance? Something came up in Grant's schedule."

She hesitated as Chad walked in with the pizza, his brow furrowed as he saw her face. It was only one day, and she'd set aside tonight to prepare. She and Chad usually went out to dinner together every Wednesday but he would understand her having to cancel. "Yeah, sure, tomorrow's fine."

"Thanks a lot for being flexible, Marley."

"No problem. Thanks for calling as soon as you knew there was a conflict."

"No problem. Take care and see you tomorrow."

Marley said her good-byes and hung up her cell phone, staring at the lit screen.

"Everything okay?" Chad said around a mouthful of pizza.

She looked up to see him holding a slice in his hand. "Can you get a plate?"

"Why dirty a plate when I'm going to polish this baby

off in five bites?"

"Get a paper plate, you filthy animal."

He rolled his eyes and stalked over to the refrigerator, where she kept a stack of paper plates on top. He pulled down one for himself and then handed another to her. She slid a slice onto her plate and then licked her fingers. "It's not that big of a deal, but they moved my interview to tomorrow."

"So one day earlier?"

"Yeah." She took a bite of pizza. Heaven.

"It's okay. We'll get you prepared tonight. You can totally do this."

She nodded, feeling weird. She wouldn't talk to Austin again until after her interview. She hadn't even had a chance to tell him about it. They always seemed to chat about random stuff while on the phone, like the new restaurant they were building out along the bypass or the latest box office figures for *Aric's Revenge*.

She had wanted Austin to be a part of this big event in her life, but they were so new. She didn't need to call him just to tell him about it. It'd be a surprise when he called her tomorrow evening.

She picked a pepperoni off of her slice and dropped it into her mouth. "You're right. I'll totally do this."

Chad returned her grin.

Austin rubbed the bridge of his nose with his thumb and forefinger.

He told himself that being at the *Gamers'* office was

okay. Marley had said she'd be out eating dinner with her brother that evening, and it was after hours, so he, Grant, and the editor James—who was in his own office—were the only ones in the place.

"Where's Sydney?" he asked, antsy to get out of there.

Grant waved a hand toward the door. "She's off getting a drink from the vending machines in the lunch room."

She'd shadowed Grant that day for a school project, and Grant had asked Austin to pick her up and give her a ride home.

"What did you say you were doing here late, again?" he asked Grant.

His friend swiveled around in his chair. "I have an interview coming in about ten minutes or something."

Austin tensed. "Who?"

Grant raised an eyebrow. "Not like you know him, you antisocial bastard, but his name is Jack Sorrel."

Marley had mentioned him. She called him a douchecanoe, which had made Austin laugh out loud. Austin picked a piece of lint off of his dress pants. He had no involvement in the editorial side of *Gamers*. He was more or less just an investor now. He never asked questions about employees or anything, preferring to observe from afar. He knew it would be odd to ask, but he did it anyway. "Do you like him for the position?"

As expected, Grant stared at him. "Uh, not sure. I think I'd rather hire the chief copy editor. She's smart and organized. Knows her shit better than anyone in this place really."

Austin had to cough to cover up his smile. His heart beat so hard, he thought it would come out of his ribs. What was that feeling? Pride. He was proud of his Evelyn. "Well I'm sure you'll find the right person for the position."

Grant was still looking at him, like he was trying to figure out a puzzle. Austin looked away.

Sydney appeared in the doorway, a diet Coke in her hand. "Hey, Uncle A."

He smiled at her "Hey you. How was your day?"

She wrinkled her nose. "Kinda of boring."

Grant made an exaggerated gasping sound. "How dare you!"

Sydney took a sip of her soda. "Dad, you played *Minecraft* all day."

"Liar."

"Slacker."

Grant pointed his finger at her. "That game is addictive, and I will have none of your lip, young lady."

Sydney rolled her eyes and then turned to Austin. "Can we stop and get dinner? I'm starving."

"Of course," he said.

Sydney hoisted her book bag onto her shoulder and walked around behind Grant's desk. "We're heading out, Dad. I was just giving you a hard time. I do appreciate you letting me hang here today."

Grant ran his hand down the long braid that hung over Sydney's shoulder. "I know. Thanks for wanting to spend time with your old man."

"You're not old."

"My aching back!" Grant wailed.

Sydney leaned down and pressed a smacking kiss to Grant's cheek. "See ya, Dad."

"Take it easy on your Uncle A."

"Always do." Sydney rounded the corner of Grant's

desk and began walking toward Austin, when there was a knock on Grant's open office door.

Austin turned around, and his stomach plummeted into his shoes.

Marley stood at the threshold, hazel eyes doubled in size. Her gaze darted to him, Sydney, Grant, and then back to Austin.

He stood frozen, unable to move. Marley wore a skirt suit, her makeup and hair carefully arranged. She looked… ready for an interview.

When Grant spoke, Austin stifled a groan. "Oh, Marley! I forgot we rescheduled your interview. Sorry, come on in."

But she didn't come in. In fact, she didn't move. She didn't hide her emotions well, either, because confusion was written all over her face, from her parted lips to the furrow in her brow.

"Hey!" Sydney spoke up. "I met you at the movie theater."

Marley blinked a couple of times before focusing on Sydney. She nodded once.

"So you work here?" Sydney asked her.

Marley finally opened her mouth farther and formed words. "Um, yes. Yes, I do."

"Oh cool!" Sydney said. "Grant's my dad." She looked up at Austin. "You didn't tell me you two were coworkers."

Austin cleared his throat, but Marley beat him to it.

"We're not really coworkers," she said, but her voice shook, like she wasn't sure she was right. Maybe it was Austin's frozen stance. He had always been so great at disguising his emotions, but his whole presence probably screamed *Caught*!

And his worst fears were confirmed when Sydney

frowned. "Right, I guess Uncle A's your boss, right? He owns *Gamers* with my dad."

The floor fell out from beneath him, and he was sucked down, down, into a basement alone. Without Marley. Without anyone, really.

He'd spent so long in that basement, and he'd been happy there. But now he'd seen what it was like up top and he didn't want to go back there.

But Marley's face was so pale, and her balance wavered. She shot out a hand and gripped the doorframe to keep her on her feet.

"Right," her voice was a whisper. Then she cleared her throat and spoke louder. "Right." And then she looked right through Austin, like he wasn't even there. Her eyes went to Grant and her voice was almost a plea. "Are we ready to get started?"

Grant was staring between her and Austin, a frown on his face. And Austin clamped his mouth shut. As much as he wanted to pull Marley into his arms and apologize and come clean about everything he kept from her, he couldn't do that. He couldn't embarrass her in front of Grant, right before her interview.

So he kept quiet, and he watched as Marley pulled herself together. The color came back into her face. She brushed her hands over her jacket and skirt, like she wanted to erase his touch.

Every cell in his body hurt. Was this what heartbreak felt like?

He licked his lips, wondering if he should say something, anything. But Marley was walking into the room, her bag clutched tightly in front of her. She didn't look at him and she allowed herself a wide berth around him to take a seat across from Grant's desk.

Grant was still staring at Austin like he wanted an explanation. But he wouldn't get one. Not now. Austin had done enough damage. There was no way he'd say anything now.

So he nodded to Grant and ushered Sydney out the door, even though his broken heart was back there on the floor with Marley.

M arley drove home in the dark in a daze. In fact, the whole last hour and a half felt like some sort of dream sequence. Or nightmare sequence. One of the two.

The man she'd been falling in love with was her boss. He owned the magazine she worked for. And not once had he thought to tell her that super-important bit of information.

And of course, she'd found out right before arguably the biggest interview of her career. An interview that she stammered and stumbled through. James had stared at her like she was ill, and Grant had spent the whole time frowning at her and then the door of his office, like Austin was going to magically appear.

If he had, she might have been hard pressed not to knee him in the balls.

He'd lied. Lies of omission were still lies. And he knew how much this job meant to her. He knew how important it was to her. He hadn't said one word about how her paychecks came from his bank account.

What else had he lied about? Did he actually care about

her? Maybe that whole story about his father had been a lie.

A voice in her head told her no, that he'd been honest about that. But the trust wasn't there. He'd shattered it in an instant. She could still see his deer-in-headlights look when he turned around. But worse was when he quickly adopted a blank expression, like he'd wiped his memory card. Of the movie theater lobby, their date, breakfast in bed.

Everything just…back to blank. Default. Factory settings.

The tears did come then, in hot streaks down her face. She banged her hand on her steering wheel, glad for the cover of darkness as she cried on the way home from the office.

She wept for her fucked up interview. She wept for herself. She wept for Austin. And she sobbed for what they could have been together.

Chapter Thirteen

Austin hated his gas fireplace. He lay on his back on his living room floor, staring at the flames, wishing for the smell of wood burning.

His builder had said it was efficient and clean. And Austin had wanted nothing but the best, because when he was a kid, he hadn't had anything close to the best.

But now, he wished for the old-fashioned brick fireplace he and his dad had had back in their small ranch house. He'd forgotten to close the flue one time and a bat had gotten into their house. Austin smiled a little at that memory, picturing his stoic dad roaring and swinging a broom wildly at the winged animal.

His back started to hurt, because there was only a thin rug separating him from his wood floor. It was not lost on him how pathetic this was. He hadn't bothered to dress that morning and only wore a pair of pajama bottoms.

He'd never brought a woman here. It wasn't even a

conscious decision. He had no set rule of *No Women in the House*. But this was his place, his refuge. He had photos of his father and plaques about *Gamers* and *Aric's Revenge*.

If anyone really wanted to know who he was, they only had to come here. It was all laid out.

With a sharp pang, he thought his one main regret with Marley was that he hadn't brought her here. He hadn't cooked for her. He hadn't shown her who he was before he royally fucked up. He'd had so many opportunities to come clean, and he'd avoided them because he was selfish. And a coward. He'd known all along she was the one, hadn't he? He'd known, and then, scared she'd leave him, he kept quiet. And his silence made that fear into a reality.

He was thirty-two years old and more fucked up than he wanted to admit.

He groaned and rolled to his side.

Stupid fucking fake fireplace.

A door opened, and the creaking signaled it was his front door, which needed some oil on its hinges. He tensed, knowing he'd locked it, and rolled onto his back.

The footfalls were familiar, though, and Austin relaxed when Grant sauntered into the room.

He stopped at Austin's side, peering down at him as he took a large bite out of a breakfast burrito. He nudged Austin's rib with his foot. "Looks like you're handling this well." His voice was muffled but still sarcastic through a mouthful of food.

Austin scowled. "Handling what well?"

Grant swallowed and cocked his head. "Heartbreak."

Austin stared at him.

"Sydney told me you had a date. You've been distracted

lately. Now you're lying on your floor like a weirdo. I put it all together because I'm smart like that."

Austin snorted and rolled onto his side, away from Grant, to stare once more into his fireplace. "How the hell did you get into my house?"

"Uh, a key." Grant's voice moved and the man came into his vision. He set a carrier with two steaming Styrofoam cups on the coffee table and sat down in a recliner. He propped his feet next to the drinks, which Austin could smell were full of coffee.

"A key."

"Yep."

"I don't remember giving you a key to my house."

"You didn't." Grant said casually, tearing off a piece of tortilla and tossing it into his mouth.

"Then how the hell did you get one?"

Grant shrugged. "You have a key to my house. I figured I should have one to yours. I made a copy from your keychain."

His friend was infuriating. "I have a key to your house because sometimes I help with Sydney. There's no need for you to have one for my house." He paused and then muttered, "I don't even have a cat."

"You could at least get a fish tank."

"I don't want a fish tank."

"Or, like, a gecko."

"Grant—"

"Did you know they sell hedgehogs now? Pet hedgehogs."

"Who's *they*?"

Grant ignored him. "I kind of want one, but Sydney said no. She doesn't trust me to take care of it. She ruins all my fun."

Austin squeezed the bridge of his nose as a headache began to blossom between his eyes. Which wasn't unusual around Grant. "Did you come here to talk about pets?"

Grant gestured to another foil-covered package on the coffee table. "I brought you breakfast."

Austin rolled to his stomach and then pushed up to standing. He sat down hard on the couch and stared at what he assumed was another breakfast burrito. His favorite coffee shop made these, and Grant knew it. It was also not on the way to his house from Grant's, so his friend had to drive out of the way to get it.

Which made Austin feel like shit to say, "I'm not really hungry."

Grant kept chewing and didn't respond.

Austin didn't really want to talk. He'd been enjoying staring into the fire, wallowing in his thoughts.

He grabbed one of the Styrofoam cups and lifted off the lid. He took a sip of the bitter black coffee.

It burned his mouth and throat and he coughed. "So, I've been seeing Marley Lake."

Grant's jaw dropped, open mouth full of burrito. "Well, shit."

Austin nodded, eyes on his hands. "Yup."

"I thought there was something going on between you when she showed up in my office while you were there. And then her interview…"

Austin jerked his head up. "What about it?" he demanded.

Grant winced. "Oh man."

Austin leaned forward. "What. Happened?"

"Calm down. Look, it just didn't go well, okay? She was a wreck. She seemed distracted and unsure of herself. I'd never seen her like that. James didn't know what had gotten into her."

Austin jumped to his feet and began pacing in front of the fireplace. "This is all my fault. Fuck!" he shouted, slamming his hand down on the mantel. He turned to Grant and held his palms together. "Please give her another interview. Please."

Grant cocked his head. "How about you start from the beginning."

So Austin did. He left out some of the more…dirty details. He told Grant about how she wanted to stay away from him at first because she was focused on her job. He talked about her ambition. How well they fit and how she made him laugh. He explained that he deceived her—deceived was a bitter word in his mouth, but there was no other word for it, really. He'd lied to her about his position at *Gamers*, because he was a selfish, distrustful bastard, and so she wouldn't refuse to see him.

"So she didn't know, Grant. She had no idea until she saw me in your office and Sydney said I owned it."

Grant leaned back on the couch and blew out a breath as he combed his fingers through his hair. "Wow, no wonder she was a mess in the interview."

"I know that I never get involved in the editorial aspects of the magazine but—"

"And you think now is a good time?" Grant's jaw ticked. "She got where she is because of herself. Not a man. And this right here is exactly what she was worried about. That you'd show her favoritism. That her colleagues would think less of her."

Austin felt helpless. "But—"

"I'm sorry, Austin. Once all the candidates have interviewed, James will pick his top choice and let me know. And that's all I'm going to do."

"But—"

"Quit saying *but*. You know I'm right. We're conducting interviews with members of her team about her leadership skills. It's not all about the interview. Which is good for Marley." Grant's eyes narrowed. "You believe in her?"

Austin bit his lip. Then he nodded. "And I…love her."

For the first time that day, surprise flitted over Grant's face. "Then she'll prove herself. One bad interview won't break her."

Austin's chest constricted. An interview might not break her, but had he?

"You need to talk to her, Austin. Do you want to be with her?"

He held his hands in front of him in a pleading gesture. "Of course, but how's she ever going to trust me again after this?"

Grant laughed bitterly. "That's rich coming from you. You want her to trust you when you don't trust her?"

"I trust her."

"Yeah? I get that you were hesitant to tell her about *Gamers*, but why didn't you tell her about *Aric's Revenge*, huh? Why'd you let her keep thinking you worked in the damn IT department?"

Austin's face prickled as the blood drained from it. "Because you know how I am. I have a hard time trusting anyone—"

"Do you trust me?" Grant's chin was raised defiantly.

"Of course I trust you."

Grant picked up the wrapped burrito from the coffee table and chucked it at Austin's head. He ducked at the last minute so it hit the mantel, knocking off one of his Aric figurines. "Hey, that was a first edition—"

"I don't give a fuck. You can get another one," Grant said, on his feet now, jovial expression gone. "And really? You trust me? You rarely put me in the position to prove to you that I can be trusted. Austin, you wrote into our *Gamers* contract that you must sign off on all major financial decisions. Then, you tell me you want to sell. I find you a buyer that I believe in, and you drag your feet, acting like we gotta waterboard Ethan or make him pay a dowry or some shit. If you trusted me, you'd quit hemming and hawing and fucking sell it!"

Grant was out of breath when he was finished shouting.

Austin swore he'd just been transplanted to another planet. He hadn't realized Grant felt like that. Not at all, and the whole thing was making him sick to his stomach. "I just want to make sure you're okay going forward—"

Grant ran his fingers through his hair and then down his face. "I know, Austin. I'm sorry for yelling but damn, you can be frustrating as hell, you know that? Jesus Christ."

Austin did know that. Which was why he held on to Grant maybe a little too hard. Grant put up with him. And Marley had, too.

Dammit.

Grant stepped forward. "I know your intentions are good, but at the end of the day, you have to trust me that I know what's right for my business. That I chose a good partner to take *Gamers* to the next level. Put a little faith in me, Austin."

He could trust Grant. He could sell *Gamers* and somehow try to get Marley back, since he'd no longer be her boss. It'd take one word, wouldn't it? One word, a signature, and a handshake.

Even if he couldn't get Marley back, he owed Grant. So with sweating palms and a shaky voice, he held out his hand. "Let's call Ethan."

Marley swiped the crumbs off of her desk into her trash can. She'd now had approximately three doughnuts today. Okay, three and a quarter if that doughnut hole counted. Which it probably did.

Owen had sensed her mood like some weird psychic and had been plying her with doughnuts all week. Which was awesome for the twenty seconds it took her to eat the doughnut, but not for the hour of self-loathing afterward.

This stupid heartbreak was going to be hell on her waistline.

She eyed the doughnut box on Owen's desk. He held it up, an eyebrow raised, and she glared at him.

She needed water. Or maybe a juice cleanse.

Marley stood up and grabbed the dusty water bottle on her desk. On the way to the lunchroom, a deep voice stopped her. "Marley."

She closed her eyes and took a deep breath. That was Grant's voice. Which, other than Austin's, was the last one she wanted to hear. Not after she'd humiliated herself in that mess of an interview.

She turned around slowly and met Grant's blue eyes. He stared at her for a moment, and for the first time ever, she thought he looked nervous. "Uh, could I have a word with you in my office?"

The way he said it sent a chill down her spine. He'd found out. He'd found out about her and Austin and here was the old heave-ho. The *we're letting you go*. The *we decided to go in another direction*.

She glanced nervously at her desk, but no one was discretely shoving her things into a box. She really, really wished she had water right now because her mouth was as dry as the Sahara.

She exhaled and then straightened her spine. She'd do this with dignity. Grant gestured to his office and she walked ahead of him, head high, white fingers clutching her water bottle.

He motioned to the chair across from his desk and the click of his door shutting was like a bullet into her ribs.

Grant sat in the chair behind his desk. He picked up a pen on top of his desk calendar and tapped it lightly, eyes focusing anywhere but her.

Awkward.

Finally Grant cleared his throat. "Look, Marley, I'm going to be honest and quick about this and let you know that I had a talk with Austin."

She felt like she'd been punched in the gut. Her whole body shook, and she cursed all the doughnuts she'd eaten because right now her blood sugar was crashing. She hadn't talked to Austin for a week, even though he'd called. And left messages. And emails.

She listened to one voicemail but his voice in her ear hurt her heart, so she'd deleted all the rest upon receipt. The emails she'd kept in her inbox unread.

"And, uh, I take it you haven't talked to him since…" He waved a hand in the room and she assumed he was referring to the moments right before her interview.

She shook her head jerkily, unable to get her voice to work.

Grant nodded his head and his eyes went back to his pen. "Yeah, that's what I thought. Don't blame you."

Marley swallowed and didn't know how to answer, so she stayed quiet.

"I've known him since college, did you know that?"

She shook her head.

Grant blinked. "Yeah, guess you wouldn't because Austin wouldn't have told you he knew me, huh?" He didn't wait for an answer. "Well, anyway, we're best friends and Austin has always been a little high on the eccentric quirk scale, you know?"

This was like the *Twilight Zone*. Was she having a conversation about her ex-lover with her boss?

"So anyway, I know what he did is terrible. There's no excuse for it. But I want you to understand that while he deceived you, he did so out of fear. He didn't want to lose you. I've never heard him talk about a woman the way he talks about you."

Marley blinked. The wounds on her heart were too fresh. They were still oozing, and she needed them to heal before she decided if she could bare it again.

Grant blew out a breath. "And I want you to know he had absolutely no say on your promotion."

That made her happy, at least. She smiled, although she knew it was a little shaky. "Thank you." That was really all she was capable of at the moment. "Is...is that all?"

Grant stared at her. "Did you hear what I said?"

Marley frowned. "You said he had no say on whether or not I got the promotion."

Grant's lips twitched into a small smile. "That's not what I said. I said he had absolutely no say on your promotion."

Her brain was usually faster than this, but now it had to push through the doughnut sludge. "Did you...are you saying I got the promotion?"

Grant smiled widely this time, showing his straight, white teeth. He stood and extended his hand over his desk. "Congratulations, Marley Lake, you are now assistant editor of *Gamers Magazine*."

She blinked at him. "But...my interview..."

Grant dropped his hand and sighed. "It was bad, not going to lie. But your previous work spoke for itself, and all your copy editors sang your praises. In the end, you were the best candidate for the job."

"I—I—" She couldn't form words. Damn doughnuts.

Grant held out his hand again. "You could shake my hand. A thank you wouldn't go amiss."

She jerked to her feet and grasped his hand. "Oh gosh, I'm so sorry. I— Of course I want to say thank you. Thank you! I don't know what else to say. I thought you were going to fire me and now you're telling me I'm promoted. My head is spinning."

Grant let go of her hand. "Why the hell would I fire you?"

"Because of Austin."

Grant waved the thought away. "No way. It's not a rule and you didn't know. You are a valuable asset to this company, Marley. I'm glad to reward you for that."

"Thank you." She was near tears with happiness and relief. She wanted to run to the bathroom where she could sob and let her mascara run in peace.

"We'll talk more about specifics later. And we'll make the announcement later this week, so keep this between us and James, yeah?"

Marley nodded. "Thank you again, so much."

Grant eyed her like he wanted to say something else. Then he nodded and sat down in his chair. When she made it to the door and placed her hand on the doorknob, his voice stopped her. "Hey, Marley?"

She looked at him over her shoulder.

"He's a stubborn pain in the ass. If you stick to your guns and never talk to him again, I won't blame you." His lips twitched downward. "But I'll be honest and say I hope that's not your decision."

Marley didn't answer as she turned and walked out of his office.

Chapter Fourteen

Marley tugged at her corset and fidgeted with the cotton folds of her skirt, suddenly self-conscious about the high slit. She had bought the pieces for her Evelyn costume months ago, before…well, before a lot of things happened in her life. Back when *Aric's Revenge* was just a video game she loved.

Back before Austin ruined it.

"Stop that," Chad said, brushing her hands off of her clothes. "You look hot, so quit fussing."

"I feel naked."

"Well, you kind of are naked."

"Not helping."

Chad snorted as they walked through the crowd at the Philadelphia Comic-Con. All around them were cosplayers—she saw a Deadpool and a Batman. A couple Storm Troopers.

A massively muscled Kahl Drogo from *Game of Thrones*

walked by and both Marley and Chad stopped in their tracks to watch him pass. The guy winked at Chad.

Marley glared at her brother. "Seriously?"

Chad pointed at the guy's back. "I will be tracking him down later. That wink alone got me hard."

Marley rolled her eyes and kept walking. Chad jogged to catch up with her. He was dressed like Spartacus—not from the movie, but from the Starz show. He said it was because he could wear less clothes. Seeing as he was only in boots and some sort of leather underwear, she guessed he was right.

He had a crown too, for some reason. It was artfully placed a little crooked on the top of his head. Marley had rolled her eyes at that too.

"So what booths do you wanna hit?" Chad said, sauntering beside her.

She sighed. Normally, this was her favorite event. She looked forward to it every year. But this year…well Austin had ruined that too. The lying bastard. Now, everywhere she looked, she saw Evelyns and Arics. Hell, she'd even dressed up as an Evelyn. What an idiot she was. But she'd put all this time into this outfit, she hadn't wanted to waste it.

She would have bailed on the whole thing, but she and Chad went every year and she didn't want to disappoint him.

She hadn't spoken to Austin for a month. He'd stopped calling eventually. His emails had dried up. She'd read them all, but they seemed full of excuses. She wanted proof he understood what he did was wrong. She wanted promises. She wanted to trust again.

And while she thought she'd made the right decision, small things continually split open that wound in her heart, which still hadn't healed. She couldn't eat scrambled eggs without picturing him walking into her bedroom with breakfast on a tray, and she couldn't wear pale blue clothes. Even though she was busy in the new position of assistant editor, Austin still hadn't left her mind. She wondered if he ever would. She wondered if she wanted him to.

Chad tugged on her arm. "Hey look. It's *Aric's Revenge*."

Aric's Revenge had a huge display, taking up most of the center of the convention. Right now, a man stood on the stage with a microphone, addressing a large crowd.

"I don't care about that stupid game," Marley hissed at Chad.

He stared at her like she had two heads.

The announcer's voice droned on. "We have a special guest here at the panel today…"

"Chad," Marley whisper-shouted, pulling on his arm. "Let's go."

"You're dressed up as fucking Evelyn but you don't want to sit in on the AR panel? What the hell?"

She couldn't explain it. The costume had felt freeing at home, but in the car on the way over, it had begun to feel like a wool scarf. She scratched and tugged at the tight fabric. She should have stayed home, because did she really belong as an Evelyn? She had thought she'd been so sure of herself, that she'd gotten over Austin and this video game's association with him.

But she hadn't. Not at all. The corset made it hard to breathe. Her hair was heavy on her back and the fake lashes were bothering her eyes. She wanted to be home.

"I can't explain it, but I—"

"So, please, for the first time ever in public, welcome

Aric's Revenge co-creator, Austin Rivers, in Aric cosplay."

Marley's hands dropped limply to her side. A roar of white noise rushed through her ears and if a stiff breeze blew through the convention, she would have fallen to the ground in a pile of leather, cotton, and hair.

Co-creator. Of *Aric's Revenge*. The game she had been playing when he…

And he hadn't thought to…

Oh my God. The fucking liar.

Had *anything* he told her been true?

She took a step back, because no way was she going to stay to listen to this man. But Chad clamped a hand over her wrist and held her in place. She tugged, and he shot her big eyes. She shot them right back.

And then that voice hit her right in gut.

"Hello, everyone."

She closed her eyes, because that voice broke over her head and oozed into her ears like honey. Her whole body flushed hot, and her belly fluttered. She hadn't even seen him yet and her body had this reaction. How had she ever entertained the thought that she was over him?

She was a fool.

He cleared his throat, and she opened her eyes. And then that warm feeling went lower than her belly. Because, praise Jesus, her Aric of the Lobby was a sight.

He stood on the platform holding a microphone, so she feasted on every inch of him. He wore heavy, knee-high boots, tight brown leather pants and nothing on his torso except a leather harness that criss-crossed over his broad, muscular chest.

His dark hair wasn't styled, so it fell in soft waves around his ears and over his forehead. He raised his hand to brush it off of his forehead, and there was a collective feminine sigh from the audience.

Oh no. Oh no no no, she could not be here. She tugged on her wrist again but Chad held firm, his eyes riveted to the vision on the stage because Austin had started talking.

"—know I have been private about my involvement in the game. At the time, I thought it was best, but I'm starting to understand that being so private wasn't working like I wanted."

His eyes flicked to Marley's and held. She ripped her arm out of Chad's grip and turned to walk away.

Except that damn honeyed voice stopped her again.

"I guess, like Aric, I was becoming exactly what I didn't want to be. Keeping quiet about my involvement in the game turned from omission of fact to lies, and I couldn't live like that anymore. I couldn't do that to my friends and the people I…love."

She sucked in a breath. And held it. He'd said *love*. Every hair on her head tingled and she could feel the heat of his gaze on the bare skin of her upper back.

She slowly stepped back on her booted heel. And turned.

And met Austin's sea-green gaze. His lips twitched up into a small smile, then he gave her a slight nod, and began to talk about the game.

She didn't move. She couldn't move. She was held prisoner by his voice, his presence, his words. Had he just told hundreds of video game fans that he loved her?

Now that her anger had begun to recede, she studied him closer. His hands shook slightly when he spoke and sometimes his voice wavered. His eyes were crinkled at the corners, like he really wanted to cringe.

She remembered what he'd told her—how he hated dressing up. How he hated conventions. How he hated attention.

Well, he'd done all three today. Had this all been…for her?

She almost turned and left, because now that the thought was in her head, now that hope had flared deep in her heart, she wasn't sure she could take the crush of rejection again, if it turned out this all had absolutely nothing to do with her.

But then Chad slipped his hand into hers, twining their fingers together. He squeezed and she smiled.

I love you, he mouthed.

I love you, too, she mouthed back.

And he loves you, Chad pointed to Austin.

She blushed and watched her Aric field questions from the crowd.

A finger tapped her on the shoulder and she looked behind her. A man stood at her back, smiling. He was dressed like a Bauer castle guard. "Are you Marley Lake?"

"Y-Yes."

He smiled brighter. "I thought so. Um, would you mind coming with me? Mr. Rivers asked to speak to you after the panel."

"He—"

"You just have to come with me, there's a private area behind the stage."

She blinked at the man. "How do I know your loyalty lies with Aric? You're wearing Bauer's uniform!"

The man's eyes widened. And then he threw back his head and laughed. The voice in the microphone stopped and when Marley looked up on the stage, Austin was glaring at them. Well, more like he was glaring at his messenger. He cleared his throat loudly into the microphone. "Are you quite done?"

Quite done. Oh, how she missed his mouth. For many reasons.

The man sobered quickly and nodded at Austin, who continued talking.

"I'm Steven." He held out his hand, which Marley shook. "Anyway, you'd better follow me before Mr. Rivers takes off my head."

Marley giggled and looked at Chad. He released her hand and waved her on. "You go. I can take care of myself. And if you don't come back to our room tonight, I'll make good use of it myself." He winked at her.

She gave him a quick hug. "I'll call you."

"I won't wait up."

With a wave to Chad, she followed Steven to the area behind the stage.

They ducked behind a black curtain, and Marley took two steps in, her boots thudding on a stone floor, before she stopped dead, then spun slowly in a circle. The entire area was an exact replica of the throne room in Bauer's castle. There were stone walls and flickering sconces. She stepped closer, noting the light was electric rather than real flames. A golden throne sat on a stone platform. It even smelled like what she imagined the throne room would, musty and cold with a tang of iron from weapons and blood.

She began at one area and ran her fingers over the wall. Real stone, with real grout. She even found a stone in the lower corner that was weakened, like the stone players used to gain entrance into the castle. It made her smile, as she sifted the dust on the ground in her fingers.

She stood up, letting the grit fall to the stone floor.

"Incredible work, isn't it?"

She whirled around, her hand quickly falling to her side. Austin stood inside the black curtain, watching her.

He was ten feet away now, much closer than he'd been when she'd seen him on stage. The light was dimmer, but his pale eyes glowed. Those pants did incredible things for his legs, showing off all the muscles in his strong thighs. She wanted to tell him to turn around so she could check out his ass.

Down, Mars, she told herself.

Her hand clutched her skirt. "It is incredible."

He glanced around. "We're going to unveil it tomorrow, when we announce we're working on a second *Aric's Revenge.*"

Well, that perked her ears. "Oh?"

He toed the edge of a stone with his boot. "Yeah, it'll be *Aric's Rein.* He's king now, having taken control of the kingdom he conquered."

"Wow. I guess you'll, um...be the creator of that one too?"

Maybe her tone carried a bitterness she hadn't done a good enough job disguising, because his head shot up. Guilt was plain in every facet of his face. "Marley—"

"It's okay, I shouldn't have said that—"

"No, you should have." He took a step forward. "You have every right. I know I fucked up..." His voice trailed off. "I have a hard time with trust. I told you about my mom leaving, then I never felt like I could rely on my father so when he stole money from me, it really messed me up. I kept things from you I shouldn't have." He rolled his lips between his teeth. "I should have told you about *Aric's Revenge*. If I had, it would've meant admitting I trusted you. That you meant more to me than I had originally thought. And it scared the shit out of me."

His words were like arrows through her anger, piercing wide holes in it until she could barely see it anymore. "And *Gamers*?"

"I'm so sorry. I didn't tell you because, at the time, it didn't matter. I was never involved with the editorial aspects of the magazine. And then, when I got to know you, I didn't tell you because I knew you'd leave when I did. And I didn't want you to leave." He smiled and chuckled. "I tried to keep you in a little box in my mind. I tried to control everything about us until I realized that I didn't really have any control at all, did I?"

Marley continued to step toward Austin until she stood right in front of him. She laced her hand in his. "You did have control, but you had it because I let you. Because I wanted it."

He brushed her hair off of her shoulder and cupped her neck. "You refused to stay in your box."

It was her turn to laugh. "That should go on my résumé."

His face sobered. "You have to know I had nothing to do with your interview. Or promotion. Or anything. I was in Grant's office because I was driving Sydney home. And I sold my half anyway."

"You sold it?"

He nodded. "I've been planning to do it for a while, but I'd put it off for…well, a number of reasons that Grant made me face…and you. So I sold it."

She squinted. "I had something to do with your sale?"

He blushed. It was adorable. "I knew I was going to have to tell you eventually. I thought maybe you'd be less angry if I could hedge it that I'd sold the magazine."

"I would have still been super pissed at you."

"I didn't say it was a good idea."

She pressed her lips together and he lowered his head until their foreheads touched.

"Please forgive me. I'll be honest now, one hundred per-cent honest, that I did this for you. I wore these pants that are chafing my thighs and this god-awful harness and I stood up on that stage for you, my Evelyn. Without me knowing, you'd worked your way inside and ransacked my heart. I miss you, and I want you back."

He said the words against her lips, so his every exhale was her inhale. The sincerity of his words spread through her body like vapor, weakening her joints until her whole body was jelly.

And then he said three more words that shredded every single doubt she had left. Those sea-green eyes looked deep into hers and his hand on her neck tightened. "I love you."

She did the only thing left to do. She rose onto her toes and pressed a kiss to his lips.

Chapter Fifteen

The first sensation of Marley's lips on his was like a drop of color in a gray world. His entire body flushed hot. His heart beat in his ears, and he swore he could feel his heated blood rushing through his veins.

Marley.

Marley was back and in his arms and she didn't hate him. If this kiss—her moving lips, her tongue seeking entrance into his mouth—was any indication, she forgave him, too.

He clutched her waist, digging his fingernails into the leather corset, frustrated he wasn't touching bare skin. He skimmed a hand over her hip and down her thigh until his fingers touched flesh. He pulled back from the kiss and glanced down. His hand was on her thigh, where the slit in her skirt separated. "This is fucking sexy, Evelyn."

She pressed herself against him, her hands teasing at the leather harness on his chest. "I had to show my Aric I still had it after being held captive for years."

He laughed. "Oh, sweetheart, you still have it."

She grinned at him and, fuck, he'd missed that cheeky grin, the one where she knew she amused him.

He leaned in for another kiss, starting slow, but with intent. He wasn't messing around anymore and if he knew Marley, she'd follow his lead.

She did, opening her mouth with a small moan as he delved inside. He began walking backwards, and even though Marley's skirt twisted in his legs, he maintained his balance while still kissing the hell out of his woman.

When his calves touched the back of the throne stage, he stopped and pulled out of the kiss. Marley blinked her eyes open, her cheeks red, that beautiful flush creeping down her neck. He ran a finger along the edge where her corset met the skin of her bare breasts. He licked his lips and glanced behind him, then he stepped up onto the stage. He bent down and held a hand out to Marley. "Join me, my lady."

She stared at him, then the throne over his shoulder. Her breath hitched and she glanced around the room. "Austin—"

He beckoned with his fingers. "I promise you, no one will come in here."

She narrowed her eyes, but they were glassy and full of lust. He knew he had her. "How can you be so sure?"

"Trust me," he whispered. "No more lies."

Her chest rose as she inhaled a deep breath and then exhaled slowly. Her mind was working behind those eyes; he could see it. Then she nodded, as if she'd come to a decision, and took his hand. "Okay, then."

He helped her onto the stage and wrapped an arm around her back, curling his hand around her waist. He swayed her slightly, so her skirt swished around his legs.

"Did you miss me, too?" he asked, not bothering to hide the vulnerability he felt.

She gripped his biceps and stared up at him. "Yes. It's amazing how many things reminded me of you. And I wasn't sure I wanted that to stop."

"You didn't take my calls."

"I wasn't ready." She dug her fingers into his muscles.

"And you are now?"

She raised a hand and cupped his cheek. He turned his head to brush his lips over the heel of her hand. "I'm ready for my heart to stop hurting. I'm ready to stop missing you. I'm ready to start us again."

He pressed a kiss to her lips again, as her hand shifted to the back of his head and tangled in his hair.

He turned them around quickly and pushed her onto the padded throne. He knelt in front of her, and her eyes widened as his hands skimmed up her bare calves. "What are you doing?"

He pushed her legs apart and she sucked in a breath. She wore a small, nude thong, which was perfect for what he had planned. He grinned up at her as he made small circles with his thumbs on her inner thighs. "The new king only kneels for his queen."

"Austin—"

He hooked her knees over his shoulders and slid her butt to the edge of the throne. Then with one finger, he pulled her thong to the side and spread her open. He blew gently on her exposed, glistening pussy and she jerked. Instead of his name now, she moaned.

"I missed this sight, Evelyn. Missed your sounds."

She arched her back and gripped his hair as he blew a

stream of cold air on her again.

"I love how you spread for me, sweetheart. Do you want my mouth?"

"Ausssstin," she hissed and he smiled. "Yes."

He leaned closely so she would feel his hot breath on her sensitive skin. "Say the words, Marley."

She gripped his hair tighter. "Please, Austin, I want your mouth."

"As my queen commands." And then Marley got his mouth. She cried out and he reached up, sticking two fingers in her mouth because while no one would come in, her shouts would be heard outside these walls. She closed her lips around his fingers and sucked as he fucked her with his tongue and swirled around her slit.

He missed her taste and her moans. He missed her surrender of control. He missed *her*, her laugh and smile and dirty mouth.

He missed all of Marley, and now she was his again. Her taste was only for him; her surrender was only for him.

She was all his.

Marley began shuddering and he knew she was close. He pulled back before she could come and stood slowly, staring down at Marley, whose skin was covered in a flush. She stared up at him, bare and beautiful.

Swifly, he picked her up and took her place on the throne. He set her on his lap so she straddled him. Her hands were everywhere, almost frantic to touch and taste. She sank her teeth into his neck as he dug in the tight pocket of his pants for the condom he'd placed there. Wishful thinking that was now a reality.

He unlaced the front of his pants with fumbling fingers

as Marley started nibbling along his collarbone. She was grinding her hips on top of him, madly seeking release and, fuck, he wanted to be right there with her.

He finally pulled his hard cock out of his pants and rolled the condom onto it. He looked into her eyes and slapped his palm down on her outer thigh. "Ride your king."

Her eyes went hazy, and when she sank down onto him, he swore this was heaven. She gripped his shoulders, digging her nails into his skin as she rode him hard. Her bare ass slapped against the leather of his pants, the sound erotic as it bounced off of the stone walls around them.

He pulled her close and shoved his face into her cleavage, licking at her skin and abrading it with his teeth.

It had been a long time since he'd been inside Marley, so he could feel the orgasm coming, quickly. Marley's breathing was labored, her head thrown back so he knew he could get her there with him. He reached between them and pressed his thumb against her clit, rubbing that button between them. Marley gasped, her fingernails sharp on his skin, and then she was coming. He slapped his hand over her mouth after the first shout, so every other cry was muffled. When he came too, with a blinding crash, he shoved his face into her neck and bit her skin to keep quiet.

He unlatched his jaw but kept his face pressed against her, breathing her in and appreciating her warmth. Her arms came around him, cradling his head.

A soft kiss landed on his temple. "I love you, Austin, you secretive bastard. I love you."

He might have cried if he was that kind of guy. He raised his head, pulling her even tighter against him. "I love you, too."

When they pulled themselves together as best as they could, which wasn't too hard since they weren't wearing a lot of clothes to begin with, they left the *Aric's Rein* set. Marley had never seen Austin this relaxed. He walked quietly at her side, his fingers laced loosely in hers. Even when they were intimate, he had sometimes seemed tense, like he was taking everything too seriously. But now, he was loose-limbed and calm. She liked him this way.

And she loved his words. She loved them a lot. She hadn't wanted to forgive him for his lies because she thought that might make her seem weak, but as time went on, she wasn't so sure anymore. It took strength to forgive.

A man dressed as Breck was standing outside of the set. Marley recognized Aric's right-hand man by his blue tunic, easily spotted in the game. When he turned, Marley realized it was Grant. His blue eyes shone as he took in their rumpled appearance. Marley immediately colored. She wondered if he'd heard anything.

"Well then," Grant said, eyes on Austin. "Now that I'm off guard duty, I think I'll be on my way. I noticed a really hot Sari who I would like to get to know." He cleared his throat and winked at Marley. She smiled. Sari was one of Evelyn's fellow captives, whom Breck helped save in the game. There was a cheat code to unlock a small game where Breck fights Sari's evil brothers to gain her hand in marriage.

Grant's gaze darted between the two of them and he waved at their joined hands. "This, I approve of. Glad Austin pulled his head out of his ass."

"Run along, Grant," Austin said, but Marley heard the amusement in his voice.

Grant grinned. "Right, well you two have fun." And then

he was off.

Marley watched Grant fade into the crowd and then turned to Austin. He pulled her into his arms and she laid her palms flat on his chest. "So what now?"

Austin's face was relaxed, the normal tension lines between his brows now smooth. Marley reached up and ran her fingers over them.

"Well," Austin said. "I say we get some sustenance and then retire to our bedchamber for the rest of the day."

"Oh?" she feigned ignorance. "And what shall we do there?"

Austin grinned, his eyes full of humor. He leaned down and touched his nose to hers. "The King and Queen have important matters to discuss privately."

She nipped his bottom lip. "Such as?"

He pressed his lips to her ear. "Such as how many times the Queen can come today."

She shivered, and smiled from ear to ear as Austin gripped her hand and led her through the crowd.

Epilogue

Marley glared at Chad. "Will you get up? Austin said he'd be here at six-thirty, which is in five minutes and we all know the man is nothing if not prompt."

Chad didn't move from his reclining position on the couch. "But this is my favorite episode."

"Yeah? Well, happy birthday and Merry Christmas, *Friends* is on Netflix now. So go home and watch it there."

He grumbled but stood up, stretching his back and scratching his belly. "Where's the stud taking you tonight?"

"I'm not sure." Marley picked up Chad's empty water glass and carried it into the kitchen to leave in the sink. It'd been three months since Comic-Con, and she and Austin were inseparable. Austin seemed…younger, happier…than he'd been when they first met. Grant confirmed this change, and told her if she broke Austin's heart, he'd smash her original SNES she still owned.

Them were fightin' words, but it was okay, because

Marley intended to care for Austin's heart like it was her own.

Chad followed her into the kitchen. "Not sure?"

She shrugged. "He mentioned dinner and a movie."

And just on time, her doorbell rang. She shooed Chad toward the door, which he opened with a smile. He grabbed the bouquet of flowers out of Austin's hands, sniffed them, then batted his eyes coyly. "For me? You shouldn't have."

Austin just stared at him, which was Austin's usual method of dealing with Chad. Marley thought it was hilarious to watch the eccentric Chad try his damndest to get a rise out of Austin. But her boyfriend managed to maintain a passive expression despite her brother's antics.

Totally hilarious.

Marley grabbed the flowers out of Chad's hands and shoved him out the door.

"Have a good time lovebirds!" he called over his shoulder.

Austin stepped inside and she shut the door behind him. "Sorry about that."

His eyes took in her clothes, which weren't anything fancy. A summer skirt, tank top, and sandals. She'd pulled her mass of hair halfway up on her head. "You look beautiful," he murmured softly, in that reverent way he had. She loved it.

"Thank you. So do you." He did, too, in a pair of jeans and a thin button-down, the sleeves rolled up to his elbows. Of course, Austin was always handsome, with that dark hair and his unusual eyes.

She'd even complimented him on the silver streaks in his hair. She thought he'd be vain about it, but instead, he'd seemed to preen under her words.

She placed the flowers in a vase full of water and turned back to Austin. "So what are we doing tonight?"

He hesitated, his gaze sweeping her body again. She looked down. "Am I not dressed appropriately?"

"No, no," he held out a hand. "You're dressed fine. Perfect. Or…" He ran a hand through his hair. Marley tilted her head. Was he… nervous?

With an odd twitch to his lips, he pulled something out of his pocket and set it on the island counter of her kitchen. "I have something for you."

It was a small square box, black, with a red ribbon. It looked a lot like…. Oh God, was he proposing? Already? Holy shit, they hadn't been together that long and… She was hyperventilating. She needed a paper bag. Or something. She placed a hand on her chest.

"Marley?" He was beside her now, a hand on her elbow. "You okay?"

"Austin this is…" Breathe. In. Out. "We haven't even moved in together yet. This might be too soon, I think. I'm not saying no, I'm just…" She was fucking this up. Her own proposal.

Austin was frowning at the box, then at her, then back down at the box.

Then, like a light bulb, recognition dawned on his face.

And he started laughing. Like, full on, clutch-his-belly, double-over-with-cramps laughter.

While she was standing there having a heart attack. "Austin!" she hissed.

He was still laughing, one hand braced on the counter.

"Austin! What the hell?"

He stood up, wiping his eyes, the chuckles still rumbling

from his body. "I'm an idiot."

She touched his arm. "No, you're not an idiot, I—"

"Marley, please open the box."

She paused. "What?"

He was looking at her intently now. "Please open the box."

She frowned, but did as she was told. She untied the ribbon, opened up the lid of the box, and there, nestled in the box, was a key. And beside the key was a thumb drive.

There was no ring. Not one glimpse of a diamond anywhere.

She smiled. "Oh my God. I'm the idiot."

He shook his head. "No, I am. I didn't even think about what the box looked like. I should have but—"

She laughed, snorting as she clutched the key. "We're both ridiculous."

He cupped her face, his grin wide. "Yes, yes we are."

She held up the key. "So is this asking me to move in with you?"

He nodded. "I want you with me always, Marley Lake."

"I want to be with you always, Austin Rivers." She loved her apartment but Austin wasn't here. And she wanted to be where he was. "And this?" She held up the thumb drive.

Austin took a deep breath. "That, to me, is probably a bigger commitment to you than a ring. On that thumb drive is the access code to a demo of *Aric's Rein.* I'd like you to play it and tell me your opinion."

She almost dropped it all on the floor. In her hot little hand, she held a demo to the most highly anticipated game of the decade. And she slept with the amazing man whose brain created it.

To Austin, this was huge. This trust he was placing in her. He was right—this was bigger than a ring or words. This was everything to him. His creation.

And he was letting her be a part of it. She gripped the thumb drive and key and brought her fist to her chest, over her heart. "Austin."

"Yes?"

"I love you."

"I love you, too."

"And Evelyn better sooo kick some ass in this game."

Austin laughed, loudly, the sound echoing off the walls of her apartment. "Oh she does, Marley. She does."

Acknowledgments

So, this book all began with a conversation with my husband. I called that stupid little spinning thing on my Mac a "rainbow wheel" and he had to go all SNL IT guy on me and tell me it's a "beach ball." I just about cried laughing that he felt the need in his nerdy little head to correct me on that.

So I wrote a page of this book starting with that. And then Marley kept talking to me. And then Austin wanted his voice heard (demanding bastard), and then before I knew it, I had this book, and I really freaking loved it.

The good thing was that my critique partners—Natalie and Amy—loved it too. And then my agent loved it. And then we found an editor who loved it just as much.

Marisa Corvisiero, as always, you give me so much inspiration to follow my dreams. Sometimes, when I don't believe in myself, you still believe in me, and that gives me the extra push to find my feet again and keep going.

Heather Howland, THANK YOU. Thank you for your

phone calls, your time, everything you put into this book. You know books and writing, and your talent as an editor blows me away. I learned so much during a two-hour phone call with you. I can't imagine how much more I'll learn by the end of this series. You encouraged me to write Marley, and tell Austin's story, and I just can't thank you enough.

To my Mobsters—I love you guys. I shared bits of this book with you while I was writing it and you were SO EXCITED. It gave me the desire to keep writing and move on and give Marley and Austin that HEA.

Tumblr was a huge inspiration for this book, I mean, HELLO, just read CHANGING HIS GAME and you'll see why. Can I thank a social media website? Whatever, I do what I want. Thanks, Tumblr!

To my husband—your nerdiness (I don't think that's a word) was such a source of inspiration to me. Thanks for answering me honestly when I inquired, "What are some technology innuendos"? Because, really, there are a lot. Thanks for humoring me in this crazy business and for loving me for what I do. Thanks for playing LEGO with the kids when a scene hit me and I had to stop everything and write.

To my friends, my family, Lia Riley, Lucas Hargis, and the '14 debuts who ALWAYS keep me sane, I couldn't do this without you. And last but not least, Andi, you'll never be one of the "little people."

About the Author

Megan Erickson worked as a journalist covering real-life dramas before she decided she liked writing her own endings better and switched to fiction.

She lives in Pennsylvania with her husband, two kids and two cats. When she's not tapping away on her laptop, she's probably listening to the characters in her head who won't stop talking.

For more, visit www.meganerickson.org or sign up for her newsletter at eepurl.com/KNN9P

Printed in Great Britain
by Amazon

74854365R00125